To help readers outside Australia appreciate the
full significance of this story, it may be necessary to
explain that there is a National Service act in force:
i.e., all young men reaching the age of twenty between January 1 and June 30, 1970, were required
to register for National Service by February 2, to be
selected by ballot (based on birth dates) for call-up.
Readers may also need to be reminded that the sea-
sons are reversed in the Southern Hemisphere, and
that in the Higher School Certificate exam, held in
Australia in November, a pass at matric standard
qualifies students for entry to university.

Thanks are due to John Murray (Publishers) Ltd.
for permission to reprint lines from "Pot Pourri from
a Surrey Garden" from John Betjeman's *Collected
Poems.*

COPYRIGHT © 1970 BY J. M. COUPER

ORIGINALLY PUBLISHED UNDER THE TITLE

"THE THUNDERING GOOD TODAY"

LIBRARY OF CONGRESS CATALOG CARD NUMBER 70-163166

ISBN 0-395-12754-8

PRINTED IN THE UNITED STATES OF AMERICA

FIRST PRINTING   C

J. M. COU

LOTT
IN LIV

Houghton Mifflin Com

1640720

Le vierge, le vivace et le bel aujourd'hui . . .
                              Mallarmé

1

LIMP HAD THIS peculiar notion of all past time being
spread around him at any particular moment. He
must have brought it with him from overseas. It wasn't
the homegrown article, that. Once Limp tried explaining it to the history master, but the history master said
it wasn't in the syllabus, and Limp shut up. Hell, I
couldn't cotton on to it either, and I wasn't blasé yet.
But for the years I spent as Limp's mate, I might never
have cottoned on. I was eighteen months younger,
and slow, and disadvantaged. But he was my destiny
and it was my future fortune I was friendly with. Now
I've got what he meant, because I liked him, seemingly. If an idea goes deep, sometimes you come at it
best through the love of a person, through your friends,
through the posture of their lives and the way they
treat you. If an idea is any good, it's sure to be acted,
Limp said. There's no good just leaving it as an idea.
There's far too many addled ideas, Limp said.

He ought to have known, for he sprang from the
middle of Europe, the Hungarian Revolution of 1956.
Here ideas keep addling by sheer inveterate neglect
and a good climate, but over there they can addle by

agitation, too. A kind of Abraham his father was, with his own Ur of the Chaldees tucked away on the Danube somewhere, and he'd risen up at the sound of the Soviet tanks and left country and kindred and all that he had, and come with his wife and one small son to Sydney, seeking harbor. And we gave him it. And the Lord must have blessed him, for he prospered, if not as the sand of the sea for multitude, still he sent Limp to our school, where the fees were pretty steep, judging by Dad's intermittent moanings about them.

They weren't on the map, Limp's lot: Dukhobors, or something; oh, I don't know. All I know is it was mighty queer meeting up with folk that lived familiarly with a knowledge of the Bible, and going in and out with them and supping with them, till you found the words beginning to dog you, too, in all the leathery healthiness of your sin and skin and perversity. And another queer thing was that they should be so clever. Benighted as they were, you might have expected an incorrigible stupidity, but it wasn't so. They kept surprising me into a knowledge of my own brains.

Limp, for all he was young, had suffered far too much in his life, so that sometimes he felt he had no right to be walking about, that the chances were against it. And soon, too soon, there came that August holiday when in some vagary our families went to the same place in Brisbane Waters, and I kept with him, on the sand, handy to the jetty, waiting into the night to see if they would fetch his father in. But they didn't: he's still in the sea. He didn't escape the Russian tanks for long and the currents of the Hawkesbury proved too Communist for him.

The turn of the tide that winter night was at 11:15, and all the lifesavers and the fishermen were deep and dependent about the turn of the tide. It was a secret stirrer, and the shoals would move in the sea and things that were down would come up, and float for a time. Limp was crouched on the beach, clear of the jetty and the small crowd, scratching in the sand, rubbing the sand out, saying little or nothing. And yet his mother was beside him, hunched, and very still and staring, and the two of them had retreated, and sometimes I heard them mourning in a lingo of their own. I acted as their lieutenant, bringing them news of the intentions of the sea. Sometimes I wrote in the sand as well, or prodded it, and dug. There were lights on the water and the sleepy sound of an engine warming up the distance at half throttle, changing its place. The plovers up at the golf course kept circling and circling around their slippery cry. Other lives were going on distinct from our lives, the Kilcare peninsula poking insensibly along the horizon, the lights of Pittwater and Palm Beach, the stupefying sphinx of Lion Island making neither sense nor sign, but just forever there.

I would have been sixteen then, I suppose, not really fit to cope with sympathetic matters, but then in my ignorance they forgave me and were kind. At the time the thing that horribly bothered me was the stammer that Limp developed. If ever he was asked to read anything in school, the words got bottled in him and he always made a shameful hash of it, beginning everything over and over again. I was the youngest in that form, felt it a privilege to share beforehand in all the breaking of voices and breaking of more elderly wind, and to be sharper in memory and languages and history than the hairy-faced earnestness in the other desks. Except for Limp, who beat me hollow; and it made me insecure to hear him crumble into stuttering. Nervousness, in any case, is the thing you especially get when you're forced ahead of yourself in school. You haven't got the judgment to know that it's judgment you lack. You've got to take everything for true, and it's lucky if you have enough retentive intelligence to hold it and put it all in place and profit by it a year or two after you were taught it. It only delays you, really. But I didn't know that till now, and I'm twenty.

One night after Limp's father drowned, we were talking away, no stuttering then.

"Must have been hard on you, Limp, to come back to school at all?"

"Yes," Limp said. And then after a bit, "But how do you mean? There were far harder things than that."

"Oh, I was just thinking of the cost of it."

"Oh, that," said Limp. "They were pretty decent. Wiped all the fees, you know. And Mum wouldn't hear of me leaving school."

"Oh, well — "

"We manage," said Limp, telling me to mind my own business like a good kid. And then he thought better of it. "Come in and say hello to her, won't you?"

Actually, I'd been looking in quite a lot in these weeks. I was shy of it, of course, awkward as a kookaburra in the things I blurted out, and I didn't even get my tongue around her name properly: but here she

4

was in a strange country and she was . . . well, she was my pal's mother and it was a hell of a thing if I couldn't — if I couldn't say a friendly word to her now and then, in the distress she was in. There's me nearly stuttering myself, in the name of God. You feel foolish talking to women who are dislocated in their language and lives, and much older than you. I always used to feel that her feet would be sore, for she served behind the counter in a Dutch shop, selling exotic food all day. But I couldn't have asked after her feet, could I?

This night she was sitting at her reading, as Limp knew perfectly well. And he also knew that the book she was reading was the Bible, and that she was waiting for him. She had a little wizened body, like a windfall apple in the mountains, and she had arthritis, I think, and I've noticed that women with arthritis are far more cheerful than I would be if I had arthritis. She screwed her face and smiled at me as if the empty room and her dull loneliness were the most comical things in the world.

It's funny what people are likely to be doing at any particular time in the houses around you. I mean, there's people believing the television ads, or baiting fish lines in the lounge, or playing games like cribbage and piquet that even the convicts didn't play when they came here. Well, it turned out that Limp's father had governed his house in this peculiar way. He'd had them read a bit of the Bible every night. And I suppose, without disloyalty, Limp was lurking about and hoping that he could now get shut of it, that he was free to grow up Australian without remorse or impediment. Limp must have very smartly noticed that the first thing necessary to every Australian is to have no religion at all.

But, then, I told you he was clever. Not clever enough, though, to beat his mum down without a battle. She was a loving woman who had lost her husband far too suddenly and in a foreign land, and she had to cling to his ways. And who could blame her?

So altogether it was a complicated business about Limp's subtle stutter and also about his asking me in that evening.

Limp was adding my presence to his arguments, hoping his mother would see, and feel, the disintegrating effect of the fine-weather paganism we breed out here in the sun. And he went clean wrong. Maybe because I'm a very historical person myself, just as historical as Limp, and must build the character of this land on all that has ever happened to it or I can't tell what monsters we'll all become? Or because I was sorry for Limp's mum, all by herself in her struggle? Or because my profane dad, who never would open a Bible, nevertheless had always charged about the house proclaiming great chunks of it in a very loud voice? Dad also had come from over the sea — like everything else, of course, as Limp would say. And he did keep persecuting us with the irrevocable eloquence of the King James Bible, exempt from decay, until I was convinced of it myself. Not marble nor the gilded monuments of princes shall outlive that powerful language, and nothing, no other cadences at all, make English so living a tongue in the twentieth century.

That's what I said. I got excited and poured it all out

on Limp's mum's lap, and she smiled her quiet smile, and I tore at the pages till I found some of the joyful downpours of Isaiah and scattered them about the room: Then shall the lame man leap as a hart and the tongue of the dumb sing, and the tongue of the dumb sing, and the tongue of the dumb sing. Oh, can't you hear it cracking like a whip and going on cracking? Or else a verse like this: The heathen raged, the kingdoms were moved, he uttered his voice, the earth melted. Or this so very opposite one: I will be as the dew unto Israel. Even Dad couldn't shout that. And Limp was astounded, astounded he was.

"Cor blimey," he said, "I'd sooner have expected you to spout cockney like the convicts. Or Irish," he said.

"Perhaps, it's all of a punch. No, gosh, it's not. Punch, or Judy," I said, "you'll find it all in the Bible."

"And do you," he said, "draw any distinction between the language and what it says?"

"No," I said, "I don't, much." I was reckless. "It has me hand and foot. You see," I said, "I don't just want to be literate. I want to be able to wield English when I grow up, and I see that this will teach me."

"You'd better," Limp said, "pay heed to what it says. It can't be anything but vain babble and fanaticism if it doesn't hit all of its joy and hope and grief and doubt and all the rest."

"True. But, gospel or not, it's as neat with its tongue as a tree lizard."

Limp's mother got little chance that night, but she looked as if her feet were less sore and as if the room

7

were brighter. And trading verses of the Bible was a game we played on other evenings after that, helping her unwilling English, and mine.

But, oh dear, I'm a zealot, and I've let you know. It sure is a mistake. You needn't forgive me, if you don't want to. I'm not asking you to. It's just that this melodiousness is standing around as Limp said, like all the rest of the past, and we could have it if we wanted. It was the same with Liz, the very same. But it's not quite time for Liz yet.

2

LIMP'S HOUSE WAS a plain fibro place, painted green, and I'm not going to describe it any further. It might as well have been a cardboard box, for all that it added to human life. And yet if you multiply it ten thousand times, and put rabbit wire around it, and straight concrete car-runs, and a tin roof, you'll have many a far-flung suburb of Sydney. It's what makes us so ill-tempered, because we've got to look at them and they desolate the eye.

It wouldn't, after that, be fair to take you into our place, so we'll just stop in the garden, where there's trees and plenty of room, and anyhow I really prefer to be outside, don't you? We've got to go up and into this tree house, but that's still plenty alfresco for me and Limp and Rod Carlson and Perce Waterhouse at the end of the next summer holiday.

There was a sucker of turpentines low down on our back fence, and they'd grown into huge discouraging trees, and when we were younger we'd built a palatial tree house around four of them, and since it was so big a house we'd put it specially high up, just to feature its bigness. It was impossible to enter it comfortably. You had to climb up the trunk of a turpentine bare of branches, and the doorstep scraped your forehead off, and after that it tore your clothes, but once you got properly up, there was a very decent door swinging on its hinges, a roomful of leaves and grit and spiders' webs, an old possum's nest, and a library of loose comics and nude magazines. Four fellows at the end of a summer vacation, even if they've long grown out of tree houses, can be so cheesed off that they'll easily go anywhere for something to do. As well, Mum was agitating for abolishing the place, and I thought the weight of the four of us might effect it. But it didn't.

Spectator sex, hot rods, how to become a real muscle man, the Higher School Certificate, sport, the top-forty racket, comic strips — I can't help it if these are all very boring subjects, but something did happen up there in the tree house, and it might interest you.

I was greedying a pair of grinning paper buttocks when this pinging vicious sigh went over my head, and in another second another pinging vicious sigh. I'd never heard a sigh describe an arc before, but this one certainly did. I couldn't believe what I knew was true, nor yet could Perce and Rod. Their eyes were suddenly very present, taking over the job of their ears. And so must mine have been. It hadn't dawned on Limp.

"Small-arms fire — "

"We're under fire — "

"Now who the hell — ?"

Cadets were compulsory at our school, and this smart recognition seemed at last to validate all the tramping about, all the standing still. Limp's back was propped against the wall that faced the firing.

"Come over here, Limp," I said, "and quick-smart."

Limp came much more slowly: he wasn't accustomed to taking orders from me, and he resented not having noticed. Maybe he didn't believe it, but I feel he was chagrined. He looked as if he would like to catch up, if we'd kindly let him drag his feet a little.

"Can't hear anything at all," he said. "Not a thing."

But just after that we heard the snap of Mutch's air gun lower down. It wasn't singing our way anymore, and we nipped out. The first man down took station behind a turpentine and spied the terrain; the next deployed to the right among the shrubs. The sergeant major would have jumped for joy. Except that when Limp came down, and was directed with a curt nudge of my imaginary rifle to do a recce along the fence. Well, he refused to go, just stood there in the middle of the lawn gazing up at the trees. Ruined the whole operation. But gradually we stopped jutting our chins and gave over being soldiers and joined Limp on the lawn.

"It's Mutch, the new man," Rod said. "Everybody knows he's potting the birds. Has all the women het up. You should hear Barbie."

We called them all by their first names, when they were out of earshot. It amuses us that oldies have first names at all, and it impugns their right to wisdom, which is fine. We were too annoyed to concede any other name to Mutch, the new man, all the same.

"What's he potting?" Limp said, wanting to be told again.

Limp and Perce didn't come from our street. In fact, Perce needed a car to come at all. He'd only just got his license, and as a result his legs had become impossible, utterly useless, as useless as his appendix.

"Birds," I said. "I told you, too."

"Birds," said Rod — a good bloke, friendly, but decisively spare in his words.

"When, when did you tell me?"

Limp was still dragging those feet of his, surely. He was bound to remember. Lately we'd been pioneering the bush down one of the fire trails and we came on this bunch of pale blue and gray feathers around a simple corner. There was a head left, and two legs, with a ring on one of them, but nothing else at all except this fine collection of soft pale blue feathers splayed out in a kind of a plate, or like mackerel clouds beginning to fluff the sky. And this neat head and pink legs. And the funny thing was that Limp was enthusiastic.

"Homing pigeon," he said. "You can see that, can't you?" And he looked at me pretty severe: stern and wild, like Caledonia.

"Yes," I said. "A homer," I said, for he was teaching me the birds. Head round and smooth as Yul Brynner's, only blue. "Oh, well," I said, "and it's not as if they're wild birds needing any protection, is it? Should have stayed with its mates, at — "

"Of course it stayed with its mates."

"How'd you know that, Limp?"

"It's not often you'd see a single homer," Limp said.

"But — "

"Oh, stow it, Guth. Use your head. Might have been a fox?"

"Yeah. Mutch says there are foxes. Come to his hen run, he says. He's next to the bush."

"Or the peregrine? Yes, might have been the peregrine," Limp said, getting pretty excited, nearly yelling.

"Well, no," he went on, a bit disappointed. "You can see how it wouldn't have been the peregrine, can't you? That was silly. Peregrines take on the wing. And then they don't hole up in the middle of a bush trail, do they? Must've been a fox," Limp said. "Oh, well."

"You don't think it was maybe old Mutch?" I said.

"Not likely. It was eaten here, right down to the head and feet. Beyond his nature. To eat it here, I mean."

Earnest, American-type joke, coy as celluloid.

"You don't seem to care about it at all, do you? You that's as potty on the birds as Saint Francis?"

"It's the wild," he said, "the clean life, things that happen over the whole of time. In the benefit of nature."

"Oh," I said, "I see." Benefit? Benefit? I was thinking.

But I only had a glimpse of murky goings-on behind the Stone Age, and I glanced at Limp in front of me to see how he could be seeing so far back, but he looked fairly pinched and ordinary and it remained a great mystery. His insight was enormous, except when it came to things like car engines, which made him yawn, and grouse. Temporary, just temporary, he said they were. He didn't have the least notion that cars would last for long. As compared with turtles, he said, or starfish, or even the Hanoverian dynasty. And then Limp

13

was smart enough not to be seen staring down at anything he didn't understand, especially if fellahs like
Perce understood it.

"Best take the ring off," he said, "and phone the bloke
up."

So we did that, and the bloke was grateful. We
couldn't do any more for that pigeon, but whether it
was Mutch or a fox or a cat that did for it, now this day
we'd been shot at ourselves, and we weren't having our
own heads going pale and blue.

"Let's go and tell Barbie," I said.

"O.K." said Rod, but he said it in that super-courte-
ous voice that meant he didn't take to the idea.

"Would she do anything?" Limp said.

"Course she would."

Really, I didn't know, but I was comparing her with
my dad, who was nearer-at-hand and who would grunt
a good deal more, but there was no hope of confronting
Mutch with Dad. And most of his complaint, anyway,
would be directed at us for disturbing him.

"I mean," Limp was saying, "you can't expect anybody to be sort of R.S.P.C.A. about a few private birds
in the bush. Or I don't expect it much, at least."

"Think I'll have to be off, fellahs," Perce was saying.
"It's about my lunchtime."

"See what I mean?" said Limp savagely, piercing me
with disgust.

"All right," I said, "I'm going to see if Barbie's in. So
long, Perce." And I started off. "You can come if you
like, Rod."

Rod lunged after me, but only with words, as if
somebody had just jabbed him hard in the gut.

"Oh. Too many. How about leave it to you two?"

Well, in spite of them Barbie was keen.

"Hm. That sort. I know him. Bit of a bastard," she said. "And the birds can't shoot back, can they ever? A fair go," Barbie said, "is the motto of this country, handed down. Fair go, mate. Where did you say you seen him shooting? Well, it's no matter anyway. Seen 'im meself."

We were walking behind her already, on the road to Mutch's place. It made us feel considerably sappy, but ours is a friendly country and we weren't having the likes of him coming and destroying the balance of nature. Old Barbie went straight to the house and breasted him up.

"If you do it again," she said, "I'll report you to the police. There," she said.

"You beauty," he said, "ya really would?"

"You do that again," said Barbie, "and you're up for the coppers, I tell you." She didn't repeat herself, and it must have convinced Mutch.

"I see what you mean, missus," said he. "Well, but, you see, I didn't mean no 'arm. What's a few jackasses more or less? Only 'avin' a go I was, for fun. Mostly always misses, so 'elp me. It's a laugh. Reckoned nobody wouldn't mind. It'd leave you sleep in the mawnin's, leave you sleep?"

Well spoken he was and he came around a bit, too. But there was no budging old Barbie.

"You do it again and, all right, I'm off to the coppers. That'll fix you."

You wouldn't have supposed there was all that support for jackasses in this nation, would you? Most politicians have less, I know, but stray dogs, stray cats, too, they do no better. They wander around on the loose and nobody cares, or else they turn them in.

But Mutch didn't half pay attention when Barbie bawled him out. There was no more shooting up the birds, no, sir. He was new to the place, as I've said, and too noisy. It's not quite couth to hear a man's conversation four gardens away, is it? He was bored for something to do, I suppose — though he must have been fifty, old Mutch. You'd have thought his daily life would have been stuffed with problems by then, without shooting up the bush for his amusement.

But there was one thing more he said. He didn't see us out at his gate, but he sent some words flying after.

"Shootin' up a few birds, that was all. Tender young buggers like you. Should be shootin' up the Veetnamese, ya should, stead of tellin' me. Comin' 'ere and tellin' me. Up the draft, says I. I 'ad me turn an' it's come around yourses now. An' I was volunteer. Tender young huffy buggers."

He was wandering away to the back of his house and throwing the words over his left shoulder. And he spat down a primula that was looking up at him.

"Don't answer him," Barbie said.

But she walked all the way home without a word more till she said, "That'll settle him," and went up her own path without looking. It could have been that the effort had churned her up, but I had a notion she might possibly have agreed with these last words of the wise Mutch. And that's what Limp thought, too.

16

3

THIS POSH SCHOOL of ours had a big quadrangle, all laid
out in lawn and roses and stone fences and notices saying, KEEP OUT. In the middle they put a big circle with
stone seats, and in the middle of that a dirty big pedestal, with a chair, and a bloke sitting on it, thinking. It
was meant to be the first headmaster or failing that, the
first chairman, or maybe it was just Michelangelo. I
don't know. After a bit only the birds take any notice
of statues. They could have the pictures in the library
as well. All the lashings of drapery, all the red faces. I
think I'd rather be a ghost myself, and haunt people
that way. But it's how these posh places go ahead; it's
acquiring tradition. Give me a ghost for that, too. Seriously. Tradition is a great matter, and it needs some
honest-to-God inspiriting imagination.

This statue hadn't been unveiled yet, though we'd
been gazing on it plenty. All the boys had been moan-
ing about it.

One Saturday early in second term the governor
was to come and unveil it, with lots of blah-blah and
local hallelujahs. It gave Waterhouse a thought — but
it was a common thought, I'll admit now.

"You'll never do it," I said.

"Oh, yes, we will," said Waterhouse. "Why not? They'll never find out. It's simple, man. All we need is a tube or two of poster paint, very black."

I wasn't too keen, but Dad thinks he's a commercial artist and our house was packed out with poster paint. I wasn't a square, nor was Rod Carlson. And student activism, there was plenty of it about. You had to protest, about anything, if you wanted to lead and to be mentioned in the newspapers and to be as important as the latest murderer or motor victim or guy that scored the winning try last Saturday. Mildness and conformity got you nowhere. The time had come when you couldn't protest too much. And anyway, I was forgetting, for as Perce said, nobody would know who did it. We'd be real Carbonari, or Maquis, take our studies into our personal lives, a thing that's not much done.

Unfortunately, we mentioned it to Limp, just mentioned it to him.

"Pooh," he said, "that's crap."

"Then what would you do? What would you do, Limp? Go on, tell us."

"Nothing," he said. "I'm busy. Kids' stuff. Don't ever do such a fool thing."

So it was off, putting black footprints on the statue.

But as he was walking away he told us what he would do. And the more I thought about it, the more intent I got. I kept thinking how there had been all these demonstrations, marches, meetings lately, and how it looked as though the hallmark of the whole lot was fecklessness. You could make as much fuss as you liked, and for as long as you could last, then everybody went home, had a beer, and forgot all about it. Even poets had wakened from their summer dreams and stood up and recited poems of protest, or just poems, or just po, before a bloody great audience with television recordings and all, and what in the end had the commentator said? He said: And the war in Vietnam never missed a beat. I was incensed at that commentator, incensed as a stained-glass window. He'd wanted the thing done, and that's what he said, the lousy poop.

So I didn't say any more to anybody, just went and did what Limp said. Of course I knew it would cause the missing of plenty of beats. But I was involved. I'd soon be twenty myself. And the world is so stap-full of Mutches, and couldn't-care-less cynical bastards.

However, as the Friday evening wore on, and the night, I did feel anxious all by myself, and I felt the want of Limp. I tossed about and didn't sleep, and in the morning I had to go around to his place and just be with him. He, not unnaturally, showed some exasperation. He was all by himself, too, but he was studying. Only a few more months to the Higher School Certificate then.

"Are you going to stay here all day?" he said.

"No," I said, "I'm not."

But I was still miserable and didn't go away.

"Look here, Guth," he said, "what's on your mind? If it's only the function this afternoon, forget it. We've had it all before, and this time we don't have to do anything but listen to the governor, and he might even be worth hearing, and seeing. He's a splendid man."

I couldn't deny it. He was. Limp was making it worse for me.

"Look here, Limp," I said, "I have to know what you think. I've been a fool."

It clicked with him at once.

"You don't mean you've put footsteps on the statue?"

"No," I said, and he breathed with relief. "But I've done what you said."

I didn't want to defend it. I was miserable, miserable. There was this long pause.

"You think I ought to confess it?"

"Yes," he said. "Except that confession is good for the soul. It isn't any good for the statue."

"Well, will you come along with me, Limp, there's a good chap? You won't go in, of course, but I'll go and see the Head."

"Wait a minute," Limp said. "I need to think by myself."

And he went out into the yard.

When he came back, he was pretty grim, but he said we'd let it stick. Refused to tell me why. Tons of reasons, he said, and I'd complicated everything.

"But go and get ready," he said, "and we'll shoot ourselves after, if necessary. I've got to register before this year's out, and I know I don't want to. For some reason no guy, I notice, specially wants to. And we're all passionate Australians," Limp said. "And better than Mutch and his kind."

That afternoon we all lined up in the quadrangle. The KEEP OUT notices were gone and the whole place looked as easy and emancipated as New South Wales in 1841, when all the convicts were reprieved. There was an awful crowd: mothers and sisters in their biggest hats, fathers grinning till their knees very nearly showed up again, but real big-business guys, of course. The sun was shining with a cruel beauty and the thing in the center looked a mass of flags and tutti-frutti frills. I wished to God we hadn't gone on with it. I'd take all the blame, of course, if it came to that. It was my affair.

It was too late, though, and I bawled the anthems, hoping the headmaster would hear. It was a sort of alibi I was making, retrospectively. But it was too late, too late.

After two introductory piles of bull from headmaster and chairman, the governor said some very fitting words and pulled the rope. I tried to make him continue by telepathy. He was an excellent man, and I admired him, and I knew the whole show would fall on him whenever he pulled that rope. Trouble is, when acts of Parliament are more frivolous than their victims, just when are the victims allowed to be serious?

The flags fell away and at the top of the pedestal on the smooth Hawkesbury sandstone you could see the words:

NO LOTTERY IN LIVES

There was this awful silence. Everybody just staring and standing there, not knowing what to do, as if the headmaster's trousers had fallen down, and the chairman's. Coincidence can be embarrassing. And there was a sameness about them. Dignity looking for a home.

I put my finger around my collar. For it was awfully tight. And licked my lips. Thought my tongue had lockjaw. I was as shattered as anybody. Limp stood like Tenerife.

Then everybody went home. I saw little groups

after, propping each other up, girls trying not to giggle, mammas all indignation. I didn't see any more of the high dignitaries.

The following Monday the headmaster addressed the school with the utmost gravity. He brought the chairman along, like the gavel a speaker keeps handy to call a meeting to order, or maybe knock a point home. Every now and then he turned and looked at the chairman, and the chairman scowled as on stage direction, or shook his head sadly, or just looked as if his heart were in the coffin there with Caesar. The chairman had a face like his own knee. Twins or triplets he was. They were all fat and receding and weighty. And figured best on Founders' Day, at the wicket: him and his knees, I mean. He was only a comic turn.

All the boys, you could see, thought it an appalling thing by Monday. That's not any guarantee of what they thought over the weekend or what they would think in the lapse and privacy of time. When the headmaster asked the culprits to own up, it took a bit of effort to get on my pins. But, then, I had Limp to help me, and knew very well that I'd have to beat him to it. Quite deliberately, I hadn't sat down beside Limp. He was behind me. But I was perfectly certain he'd be on his feet. I just thought I could defend him, and be the usual hero perhaps, and meekly. He'd never have done it, no question.

But in the next minute we were both expelled from school.

4

"WELL," DAD SAID, "there's one good thing about it. We're saved the strain of being nice to our friends, for we won't have any."

"Oh . . ." said Mum.

"It's a clean sweep. We've put up with them long enough, anyhow, swapping Christmas cards, seeing them every six months. Now they won't come at all."

"How you do go on!"

"You can call me Robinson. We're alone in the world from now on. Like the Swiss Family Robinson. Set your chin, Mum, and get ready to knit us a wigwam. I'll mix up some war paint to daub on our faces. And you girls can each have one of my old pipes to smoke."

"Oh," Mum said. "You do go on. I can't think with you going on. How can you go on like that? Makes me feel I'm in a train, and rushing past the station we get off at."

"Good," Dad said. "It's a praiseworthy thing to say. I'll — "

"Do shut up, Dad," Robin said. "It doesn't help a bit. Can't you see for yourself?"

Dad would have been off on his own, if they hadn't kept chipping in. They're forever chipping in, these women. That Monday night I couldn't have chipped in myself.

Dad shrugged his shoulders. He's very inclined to wash his hands of teen-agers.

"Why did he have to do it?" Mum wailed.

"The alderman in him," Dad said. "Anything to attract attention."

I was sitting on the very edge of my chair and I'm squirming yet to think of it. I was sitting just on the very base of my spine and the edge of the chair was very, very hard, and I was doing all I could to make it harder. Pressing down to go through the floor, like the child, crowned, with a tree in his hand, in *Macbeth*. I was also pressing the tips of my fingers together till they turned white, patting them now and again like as they lay, and steering them the way I was going, which was through the floor. It's a thing you can't do, seemingly, unless your knees are pointing to opposite corners of the room and you're in danger of rupture. But it wasn't any good worrying about these things, with Dad wildly saying everything and Mum supplying the punctuation marks and Robin snapping everybody's head off and John patiently sitting there as though we'd all gone to the Lord Mayor's Ball on stilts and spent the evening one floor up on everybody till they all turned their backs on us.

We should have been a happy family. We had health, and decent looks, and wanted for nothing. That's leaving Dad out of it, of course. Dad was always wanting for something, certainly. I just thought he was one of those Biblical guys whose bowels yearned. Once Robin said to me it was about a school, too, but I couldn't see how a grown man would yearn for a thing like that. Seemed recessive. So I contradicted her, and she said, "Oh, shut up. You were too young. Dad's photo was in the papers, and everything. Don't say I told you. And don't speak about it."

I didn't believe Robin. Dad's face, it seemed to me then, didn't have the glazed look you needed for newspaper photographs. No, I just thought Dad had been brought up wrong. In a potty village back home where he couldn't rest because his brain was active. And then he was cussed and refused to like the city, wouldn't find anyplace else but his village where he consented to know the folk. Too bad on him, we said, he just isn't friendly. Dad kept carting about this slow resentment of his friends, said we all grew better strangers every day. A thing like that, when it gets you, spreads all over the place. It's like war, or Hollywood, or a sweat rash. You can't make peace with it.

That night he was showing the usual signs of talking himself into trouble, and I was grateful.

"Well, what do we do now? I can't think of anything to meet the case. Unless for a career in the billposting way."

"It's not funny," Robin snapped.

When Robin snapped, I had to notice how retroussé her nose was. It was broad as well as retroussé. Mum's was chic and retroussé and Robin had the worst of that bargain, but she didn't seem to mind. She was younger than Mum and preferred it that way. Her hair was wavy of its own and that made up for it. A clean, wasp-waisted sort of beauty to go with her temper. If you could have filled the top half of her with sand, she'd have made a perfect egg-timer. But she wasn't struck with the suggestion — I suppose because we'd have had to turn her backside up, but she didn't explain. They're not always too obliging, big sisters, I've noticed.

Dad just paid no heed when she said it wasn't funny. He was combing his hair with his hand, abstractedly. It was a sign of invention, usually.

"There's some pretty tall hoardings on the North Shore Line. They would keep him happy. And the governor won't ever unveil any of them, I don't expect."

"Think I'll have another couple of Aspros," Mum said. "Robin, dear, would you mind?"

Mum had been going out to work for years now, and Robin said she had to.

"Otherwise," Robin said, "there just wouldn't have been enough money. As soon as you stopped mewling and puking," Robin said, "Mum went out to work."

Sounded as though it was my special blame again. I resented it.

"I suppose even lovely-lovely you would have mewled and puked once yourself, Robin," I said. "Besides," I said, "I could puke now, looking at your awful face."

"Hey," said Robin, "you'd better not say 'puke' like that again. Horrid words you let out, all the time."

"The hell I do," I said. "Who started it?"

"Oh," said Robin, sniffing the air retroussé, "I was quoting Shakespeare, don't you know?"

And she went away shuffling her bottom from side

26

to side, the way girls sometimes do in a family. It gave her an enormous shelf of a gumboil on one side, and then it shifted to the other side, like a knee going out of joint. Try as I would before the mirror, I just couldn't give myself a gumboil that size. It was a mystery to me, till the years of discretion arrived.

Anyway, I asked Mum why she went out to work and she said because she couldn't stand Dad all day. I thought at first she was joking. Since then I've read how a woman should marry a sailor if she wants to keep on loving her husband. Dad never took to the sea, so Mum went out to work. They managed that way fine. Dad was lazy and Mum was energetic. Dad was a commercial artist, did his work at home. He must have thought a bit at his brush and palette. Mum's thinking was done spontaneously. She had to see folk and speak to them before she saw any reason for thinking at all.

There were three kids in our family, though by the time we messed up that statue, the other two thought there was only one left. Robin was the eldest — about twenty-two, I just forget. She and I sat opposite at table and our feet got mixed up — also her boy friends, whom I could never stand. They'd sit about and tell me to beat it. I didn't take to it all that much. But I had a good camera, which I'd won, and when Robin wanted a loan of that, which was fairly often, she was sweet as a drain. She wasn't too bad, I suppose.

John never quarreled with her. She admired him because he was clever, and initiated him into the younger set when he was old enough, and that might have been a thrill for them both, very likely. John was the strong silent man of the family. Stood around looking six feet tall and handsome, till you wanted something done, like algebra, or a new bit of screening for the kitchen door, or if there was a hiccup to extract from the sewing machine — well, John just stopped smiling and looking handsome and went and did whatever it was. Too capable, that was his trouble. Mum never worried about anything much when John was around.

Still, he did give up playing golf with me when I was about twelve. Because I always beat him. Up till then, I'd had to overlook a swing or two, to break sort of even. He never did that, and he got into the habit of never doing it, so when I really beat him, he'd nothing to fall back on, see. Said he was giving up the game. Thought the licking was a poor reward for all his honesty.

But you never get anywhere by strictly playing the rules, I told him. Very consoling I was, and thoroughly professional. You have to understand the rules, granted, but only so as you can see your own way around them, John. After a little of that, he was able to look disgusted at what I was saying, instead of at the licking I'd given him, so that you can't say I wasn't considerate.

You'll see how my brother's name was John. Mine's Ian Guthrie. They used to call me Anus, after my brother began doing Latin. But as I've a sense of humor and laughed at it then like the rest of the kids, the name didn't stick. It could have. It was a pretty sticky one. Now mostly they call me Guth, took my other name and made a hash of it.

28

5

HAD TO GO ON about that. Sheer escapism and nervous
hopping about. I didn't like being expelled any more
than any other guy. And while I didn't give a dried
bean for what most folk said or thought, yet the truth
is no man wants to think himself out and out unique and
by himself. I was fond of the human race and wanted
folk to be fond of me. Defiance wasn't, and never was,
my line at all. People like the governor, and Limp,
and Liz, old Barbie, and Limp's mum so lonely, Dad
and the rest of the family — I was tied fast to them all,
and I knew it. On Tuesday morning I woke very early
and went over it a lot. Of course, even then, cheerful-
ness would keep breaking through, but I was perfectly
serious and I imagined myself walking straight up to
the door of Government House and knocking and saying
I wouldn't come in but would they please fetch the
governor down for I wanted to say I was sorry.

I didn't go on with that, didn't go on with anything.
Kept thinking of Limp and what he would do now.
Before the morning was out, I was certainly going to see
him, but there was something I wanted to ask Dad first,

and it wasn't easy. I had to be sure of the answer yes. And all I was sure of was that I couldn't ask anybody any question at all.

Well, yes, there was one person. This headmaster, that had made himself seen to be done that Monday morning; this letter-of-the-law man, purging himself pure by expelling us. And yet I didn't even want to ask him questions, I felt so much contempt. A sharp, sustained raspberry to make him sweat on his swivel chair, the only one in the school, and rout him out of it, that would be the thing. Lip servant, that's what he was, a man who sanctified all that his betters did, who anticipated their doings in fear and trembling. Miserably upholding iniquity all his days, except iniquity in schoolboys. He was hard on that. They think you never see how subservient they are — because they close their doors on their obsequiousness, and send it down the phone, and table it at meetings. Yet they carry on their faces the stink of it wherever they go, and everybody knows, and no one ever respects them. When you have a poof like that to guide and steer you, you haven't any guidance at all. It's no excuse. It's how it is, and it matters. For men like that are often Prime Minister, too. Take just this one inglorious example of their ways.

There was this Waldock hood. American he was and he went to our school and he had the most flash bike you ever saw. It was close to being a car, with fins and everything, and you very near had to drink petrol to pedal it, I shouldn't wonder.

This hood Waldock was such a bonehead that he might as well have sat all day at the feet of the first headmaster on his pedestal in the quad. He'd have learned as much. Once at a football match I heard his mother talking to the housemaster about her sweet li'l boy. He was six feet tall, and broad as the road that leadeth to destruction. She talked as loud as the lines of that American bike. She was determined that the old Waldock would do Latin and algebra, because next semester, back in the States, he was due for Latin and algebra, so therefore, Mr. Martin . . . Martin saw the point all right, but he must have said — he looked embarrassed — that Waldock was kind of cut out for metalwork more than Latin and algebra.

"Oh, but Mr. Martin," said Mrs. Waldock, "Junior's quite hot on languages. You don't know Junior. I guess he did all right at Swedish when we were in Sweden and at Spanish when we were in Montevideo. I didn't understand a word myself. All those foreign bods just nattering away all the time, Mr. Martin. But Junior, he caught on. Junior's a li'l bit of all right now really, Mr. Martin. He caught on O.K. Got a big heart and a big I.Q. Li'l slow, maybe, but he gets there. Junior's O.K."

I crept a bit nearer. Martin, if goaded, could lose control. He could say what he meant if he wasn't thinking.

"Mrs. Waldock, a boy can be dumb in any language. A boy can be pretty silly in Swedish and Spanish, too."

I liked old Martin. And I agreed with him about Waldock. About knowing tons of languages, too, for that matter. It doesn't mean you've any sense. Maybe Spanish and Swedish and English and American were holding such a riot in old Waldock's head that the poor bastard couldn't get anywhere quiet for thinking.

31

Anyway, Waldock knew his deficiencies, if his mother didn't. At the Half-Yearly in June he persuaded Waterhouse, who was sitting in front of him, to show him what he'd written so far, and Waldock cribbed it. Waterhouse didn't tell me. He was a good bloke, didn't like to say no. I'd have stopped it right away. It wasn't that I cared much about cribbing, but there wasn't any limit to what that bonehead couldn't do right. He was good at not being able to do things, even cribbing. He just swept up practically everything he could see on Waterhouse's page, like a development company clearing land. Even the headmaster, even the chairman, couldn't avoid seeing through it. That headmaster saw right through things as far as the United Nations, Dad said. He said his knees were his barometer, or seismograph, or something. What he meant was: his knees knocked as soon as there was any faint political smell around. Dad's word didn't really specify whether the headmaster was a headmaster or not. It alluded to his other qualities. Anyhow, I'll just go on calling him the headmaster.

When he found out about this cribbing, the headmaster debated the matter with his usual probity and at great length. Old Waterhouse and Waldock went to see him about every time the bell rang. The Head wanted to make sure, he said, that they perfectly understood the heinousness of their crime. I'm sure Waldock didn't even understand "heinousness," with all his horse-load of languages. As for the Head: *funditor tauri*, that's what he was to trade, a slinger of bull.

While the Head was slinging it, old Martin saw how the whole school was watching and praying for something clear-cut, and he wrote a sharp note to Mrs. Waldock. Waterhouse wasn't in his house.

Hiram T. Waldock, the father of this goon, was general manager of Rumbledown Motors, quite a VIP if you hold with motors and success. He wasn't having Mr. Bloody Martin telling his wife what to do about Hiram, Jr. No, sir. So he wrote a note to the chairman and said it was rediculous and spelled it that way, too. Swedish, I suppose.

Martin had thought Waldock père or mère would come and see him. But the upshot was, the chairman descended, and Martin was fired. He was a good bloke. I could say bloody hell, too.

The headmaster performed all the time like the bridegroom in that poem *Lochinvar*:

While her mother did fret, and her father did fume,
And the bridegroom stood dangling his bonnet and plume.

Just dangled his bonnet and plume, that's all he did. I bet nobody ever heard him say peep for his housemaster. Big barnsmell, that's all. And he gave Waterhouse six of the best, to show his courage and decision.

On Tuesday morning, in bed, I was certainly comparing my actions with all of that.

6

"WOULD YOU CONSIDER teaching Limp now, Dad?"

Dad had a studio abutting the house and in the fine fresh sun of the morning he worked away contentedly, abandoned by the rest of the family, who just went on sleeping. But that Tuesday morning I surprised him in his lair, standing at the wire door peering in, scratching myself through my pajamas, abject and wretched in every way. Dad, who was caught in the quiet places of his life, laid down his brush and took it up again, began mixing his paint.

"Say that again."

"I'm very worried about Limp."

"We're very worried about you."

"Yes, but — Limp wouldn't have done this at all. Oh, he agreed, he felt the idea was true, in fact he suggested it, but he never meant to slobber it on the statue. Proclaiming it far and wide, that's the hard thing. Almost looks as if you haven't got to succeed too well. Now everybody knows, and they're shocked as dammit."

"Go on."

"And what they notice is the insolence and disrespect. They ignore what the words say. I still believe what the words say. Why, you don't pick even a football team by lottery. Nobody would dream of it. They're far too moral, the rules, drawn up and moral. And to pick soldiers that way, it's a very cynical thing to do. Grownups must all be cynical, or they'd see it. It produces young cynics, too, and how d'you like that? Cynicism, it's more infectious than flu, or the Black Death. Even if you aren't cynical, you've got to pretend to be."

"You're a funny boy," Dad said. 1640720

I tried to look funnier, to show a gratified misery, that is. For that's always an encouraging and defeated remark, in parents. I knew the best thing always was to catch my parents apart. Usually, of course, we tried it on Mum, but Dad was the right one this time, able to think what I was saying. He would tell Mum about it; and if they didn't fight out the explanations . . . Oh, well, there I am cynically voicing my own calculations, I suppose. But everybody makes them. How can you live without complication? And what would be the use of doing so?

"We're supposed to be good little political pawns, fighting, and getting killed, but if we've any political opinions of our own, and push them, we're agitators and upstarts. So maybe we've got to be. They'll make use of us to the death, but they won't listen to us at all. I've heard *you* say you hate a lucky bag conscription."

"Of course I hate it. Baffles me how any government can be so stupid. They couldn't be so stupid," Dad said, "if anybody noticed, if the people cared about running their country. If you haven't got teen-age sons, you don't give a damn who's conscripted. Folks can't begin to be disinterested in public affairs; they've lost the very meaning of the word. All the town councilors are estate agents, or every other one is."

"I mean, Dad," I said, for he was relapsing into his own corollaries and would soon be painting again, "I mean, they don't seem to see how they're teaching the violence themselves. It isn't the young who begin it. Wars, they're the violent beginnings. And there's Newton's Third Law. And it applies."

"Just what is it?" Dad said, grimly. Dad didn't like to be caught with his intellectual trousers down, and he didn't dig physics.

"That every action has an equal and opposite reaction."

Dad thought for a bit.

"It's true, man," he said, with surprise. "And yet not perfectly true. If you swing a pendulum, it dies down. But how many laws did Newton invent? Maybe they're all pretty true. Must write that one down."

Dad had this habit of chalking up memorable things on a board he had. He said it teased his memory into a trot, or needled it. He was always trying to recall what had been there yesterday, or last week. And he managed to recall it. "Pelmanism," he called that game; he was old-fashioned. But I had to be quick.

"And here, Dad," I said, "the point is that if you send Americans stirring about the world needlessly fighting and killing, you can't expect to have peace at home. Write that up, too."

36

"I know," Dad said, sharply. "But where are we going?"

"The President doesn't know it. Says there's no connection between the war in Vietnam and racial violence in the South."

"You think there is?"

"I'm sure of it."

"So am I," said Dad.

"And there's a pretty strong connection between Australians meddling in Vietnam and violent protest at home. Or anywhere," I added.

"There is. It spreads like leaky treacle. And that's why you want me to teach Limp, is it? It's all so lucid."

"Oh, no, Dad," I said. "We had to talk about that. It's all mixed up together, like heaven and hell. Look. You know what's happened to us?"

"I know," he said, with mock resignation.

"I'll have to go and see him. And I thought — "

"You should have thought sooner, boy. You never thought who would do the extricating, and you can spend a day or two regretting it now. First of all, you went to Limp himself, last Saturday morning, to extricate you. And all the poor chap did was to get in beside you, and you felt happy for the minute. I'm not coming with a spade to dig you out just whenever you say the word. I wasn't consulted beforehand. Off you go. See what you mean to do, while I think what I mean to do, if anything. It's all very well finding everybody wrong and demolishing everything. All the young violents are good at that. But have you any workable suggestions? Or suggestions of any kind? Bar any mirror suggestions about votes and places on committees, which is only a kind of conformity, asking and insisting on the chance to make the same ponderous mistakes in your turn. But off you go. I want to earn my breakfast.

"Something attempted, something done
Will earn my tea and toast."

But he went on shouting after me.

"Last night," he shouted, "you all wanted me to put on my best tie and go and reason with precious Mister Mary Ann, the headmaster. With that galoot," he said. "But nothing'll ever reduce me to it. Think first and for yourself next time," Dad said, "if you won't seek advice. And then you won't need to keep acting as if you're compassed about with so great a cloud of rescuers that you can't — "

I kept on fading around the corner. You had to, in our house. There was always some addendum to torment you from room to room and delay the proper conduct of your life.

7

———

"I've seen plenty other guys," Limp said, "just saying 'Damn it, what's the use?'"

"But, Limp, I've been talking to Dad and he might help."

"He's got you to help first. What'll you do?"

"Easy — get a job," I said, though I hadn't really thought. I was still a bit out of my wit at getting Limp expelled. "It isn't the end of the world," I said.

"We thought it was."

"What do you mean?"

"That's why we came here. Thought it was the end of the world. Now Mum says it is. The end of the world for Dad, and now for me, and so for Mum."

"I'm sorry, Limp. Oh, dear. Wish I could think of something."

I went about the room touching things and using pretty female expressions, I know. But when I got to the window a strange discovery had come and made me quiet inside. It was something I'd been alerted to, that was signaling and that I couldn't catch, as if my eye were held back, like the disciples on the Emmaus road. And now between my chair and the window, I suddenly saw. I picked up a book from the too-sunny windowsill and pretended to look it over. "Limp?" I said.

He was flat on his bed, studying the ceiling. But I could see him edging after old Barbie on the way to Mutch's place, and miserably digging in the darkness in the sand when his father drowned. Though maybe that wasn't very fair. "Limp?" I said.

"Well? What else?"

"Limp," I said, twiddling the pages faster, "you gotta do something. You don't want just to knuckle under now, Limp, do you?" And I looked straight at him, feeling relieved. I'd missed charging him with anything much, with always giving in too early.

He didn't answer right off. Gave the ceiling a green grin. Then he rolled over and curled up and stared under his eyebrows up at me.

"I won't do that," he said. "What makes you think it?"

"I'm going back to ask Dad again. He could keep your English up, I know. And it would keep you in training, of set purpose, to do the Higher School Certificate. And in all your subjects. Which you're not going to flunk now! Ten weeks away?"

"No, it won't be flunking," Limp said, "not flunking at all."

I didn't trust the sound of that, but before I could speak, he went on. "What about you?"

"Oh, I'm different. I'm off to see Dad again."

And I had this feeling of missing on a plug, as I tramped my way home, a feeling of forgetting. I wish he hadn't deflected me. It would have been better if

40

I'd turned back and asked what he wouldn't be flunking then, for I'd come quite near his mind.

But going back, it's such a weak and fussy, defenseless thing to do. And he wouldn't have told me. And he'd have had to watch me start off from his door again, imitating myself.

As it worked out, I didn't see Limp again for days. I could have gone in the evening and got him at home, but then Mrs. Limp would have been there, his mum, and I'd been once already and it was very painful. You try to be gentle, but I suppose, where your mates are concerned, their parents are always inclined to blame you for any small calamities. If you go to see them, your apologetics wear off a shade too soon, your smile becomes an ordinary one, and them still grieving. Barring hara-kiri, there's little you can do to please them. Going on chatting to Limp becomes a refined cruelty, and I'm not cruel. I'm not sure of very much, but that I'm sure of. Too timid and sensitive to be cruel. And it felt heartless to talk to Limp with his mother there, handicapped by a generation and a language and loneliness and a hard disgrace. It felt heartless because it was, and I went home. I couldn't devise any way of going back, except with rejoicing, bringing my sheaves with me, a sheaf of promise about the exams and Dad's willingness to help with them. And a snag had developed there, quite unforeseen, and I'll soon come to it.

But once Limp's mum had shown me what her hope was, shyly. Often and often it recurred to me, in private, with a strange blend of remorse and huge exaltation. I thought of it so often that I had it by heart and for a friend, and I'm not looking it up even now: Psalm 126. One night she showed me her psalm, pointing — pointing, as well, at her life and her family, and her reason for being above ground.

When the Lord turned again the captivity of Zion, we were like them that dream.

That would have been how they left Hungary and came here.

Then said they among the heathen — and that would have been all of us — *the Lord hath done great things for them.*

The Lord hath done great things for us, whereof we are glad.

Turn again our captivity, O Lord, as the streams in the south.

And you see they had contrived to get captive here? But the streams in the south are sure to turn again. Even the worst drought breaks, and it's a sign. So —

He that goeth forth and weepeth, bearing precious seed, shall DOUBTLESS *come again with rejoicing, bringing his sheaves with him.*

Bringing his sheaves with him was a pleasant thing in a young man, even in a faithless generation. And I meant to do it, and Limp too, surely. But I couldn't expect her to believe me then. So I didn't repeat it. Comfort itself has got to be judicious.

8

———

THE SAME TUESDAY of the week of the expelling, as
school was coming out, I went to look for Rod and
Perce. I wasn't going to let the chairman and the headmaster cut into my habits too completely and, besides,
I was curious about what might have gone on. They
were still my friends, though somehow or other it was
hard not to bear them a grudge, I don't know why.
They'd every right to go on being at school, if they
wanted to.

First of all, we went to this espresso bar, but I couldn't
bear it — all the flies and the dago behind the bar
would keep whistling like a kettle on the boil. One of
those very melodious Cosi fan tutti-fruity bubbly ket-
tles, too. It was unusual to hear a dago whistling in
Australia. They're generally too far from home.

Apparently the grim fact was that school was much
the same as it had ever been, as comfortably lousy as
ever. It wouldn't have made any difference if I'd
scratched my head instead of the statue. And the
statue had had a shower, and some pumice stone, and
with a bit of armpit lotion it all smelled great.

Wouldn't it bog you? Made me very nearly gnash my milkshake and all. I suppose even Einstein, when he went to America, didn't properly feel that he'd altered the balance of the globe. You could go to the moon, so help me, and inside two days nobody would be talking about it, I bet. And couldn't maybe name you the guys that had gone there. It's a waste of time, political action — must be.

Anyhow, after telling me that, Carlson and Waterhouse subsided into saying nothing, in case they stumbled on even more noisome news. I had to say something and out of sheer chagrin I said it was noisome and the word was too much for them — stank them out. They hadn't much judgment between them. They just sat staring and groaning and sucking their teeth and shifting from buttock to buttock. And they gave birth to nothing. I was so provoked I couldn't give them the history of what I'd been doing myself, and they didn't seem even blankly deprived of it, and disappointed.

"Anybody got a cigarette?" was all Rod ever said.

And Perce said even less. He said, "No."

"Stacks of cigarettes behind the bar," I said.

But they only began staring again, and of course sucking their teeth, and shifting from buttock to buttock, till I was paralyzed with their repertoire.

"Look," I said, "let's get the hell out of here." I made it my courteous last request.

This dago had also one of those terribly eyebrow-penciled mustachios and, with Rod and Perce so hyper-communicative, I wanted to raise the hackles of it if I could. So I snapped my fingers as I passed and gave him the fruit. He didn't need to take it if he didn't like it. It was just that we were three little boys from school and acting up to it. Brute adolescent, it's what they expect of you. There was a TV set crouching above the entrance door and, as we went under, a woman was demonstrating a perfect genius of a washing machine. She smiled as we went past, and I snarled "Imn" and bared my teeth and gave her the V sign. And she took it with another smile. Makes me want to bawl like a rhinoceros. Strangers smiling to each other like that. She could keep all the washing machines in Arabia, as far as I was concerned.

We went and sat in the park. And then they went home and I wanted to see Liz Carlson. She was Rod's sister and what's more she was my girl friend, or was going to be. That's reckoning by my sister Robin, who kept telling me that Liz had a crush on me. But all the girls have, I said, and Robin abused me. It's very flattering, but Liz sure disguised it very well, if it was so. Some girls might have enough savvy to wait, though, till you had an interest in them. I couldn't tell, and it got me thinking about Liz. Sometimes I asked her advice on things, or else we discussed Rod, as the common link between us, or school texts, but that was finished now. Liz, I noticed (different from the other girls), didn't expect you to howl and chortle and guffaw over pointless stories around and around about what Miss Brown said, or Mrs. Whosymeflip, for nothing craps me more.

I knew she'd be with that hen-witted galah Sue Luker, and sure enough she was. They came up, all pretty juvenile in their school uniforms, knees, thighs, and straw hats. I didn't mind the knees and thighs, but those straw hats! Liz actually didn't say anything but looked uncertain and tried to smile. A bit wan they were, but resolute that I was still speakable to. Only Sue had looked around to see who would be spying out our collision, but then she was the most detachable of the three of us.

" 'Lo, Romeo," said Sue.

"Look, Sue," I said, with deplorable vehemence, "I've something to say in your ear."

She held her ear, too, so as I could say it. Sue was all impudent for confidences. There's nothing so fetching as a woman's face gone sideways and exciting as the deck of a ship — if you want to bite her ear, that is. I could have bitten Sue's, only there was the certainty of biting some of her mousy hair as well, so I didn't. I just located her ear, and said, "Pee off."

It wasn't a nice thing to say so I added, ". . . Sue."

It didn't sound too objectionable, because I wasn't being objectionable.

She was horrified. But that wouldn't have mattered so much, only Liz heard me. And Liz was real annoyed.

"What *did* he say, Sue?"

"Oh, I couldn't ever say it again, Liz," said Sue, and she shook her head solemnly. "I think he's a nasty horrid type. I wouldn't ever say such a thing to you, Ian Guthrie."

Which just shows you how stupid Sue was, doesn't it? Retaliation was the only answer she could have thought of.

"I should think not," I said. "It's not for girls at all. But I only said 'Be off!' I don't know what you're going on about. You must have misheard me. I'm a Welsh-man by descent, of course, and sometimes I get my peas and beans wrong. It's a throwback, or congenital, or something — next thing to a stutter or a Hapsburg nose."

It helped a bit. They opened their eyes and closed their lips, the way girls do when they see through the whoppers you're telling them. The knack of it is to tell a real resounding good one. You don't know whether they'll explode into laughter or protest, and as soon as any doubt shows up, you've as good as won. I like girls. Mostly you can't be of any use to them without a little awfulness in your language. At least, not now. There's a borderland that everybody's crossing and recrossing, and it has to be so with love, so that it can remain a kind of undiscovered country.

The girls' eyes were twinkling and I do like that.

"Bold as brass," Liz said. "You don't know the first thing about talking to girls."

But I didn't believe her.

"Ah well, Liz, maybe they won't want to talk to me anymore now?"

"I don't know," Liz said, quick to melt. "They're all talking about you, anyway."

"They think it's a big thrill," said Sue, as if she didn't.

"We don't," added Liz. She looked into my face, then dropped her eyes. "I suppose you had to do it?"

"Suppose so. Maybe it was impulsive. I don't know. I sure believe what it said. It's very disappointing to grow up and find that adults aren't wise at all, but just as silly as they like. They're so — well, so expedient with other people."

47

"What does that mean?" Sue said.

"Oh, how should I know, Sue!"

"You know what I mean. They're making use of young men. It isn't a crisis and they only need a few of them, a very few. Butchered to make us pals with the President. We're perfectly bloody at foreign policy. And folk don't even think about it. It's as Carlyle said: *The May sun shines out, the May evening fades, and men pursue their business and pleasure as if no young fellahs were dying in Vietnam.*"

"He couldn't have, he couldn't have said that," protested Sue.

But I'd read the first two pages of *The French Revolution* and he very nearly did. Besides, it was Liz I was talking to and looking at. Her anxious face.

"How very sad it is," she said. "Almost everybody is heartless about it. We all are. As if they were tin soldiers. What does Limp mean to do?"

"Oh, that," I said, and I pretended not to understand. I didn't want to discuss it with Sue. Liz meant about the call-up. Because Limp had come from Hungary, he'd missed a school year. Was already nineteen, had to register. It's what was in my mind, too, but I sheered away and said bitterly: "What does it matter? You can walk away from your deeds, like a bank robber. You don't care for anybody and nobody cares about you. You can be as rude as you like and you can still make a living. It's life that's defaced, not statues."

Quite viciously, I kicked at the stones on the path. We were walking home, and when I looked up again Sue had stolen away. They must have made their

48

own signals, and parted. Girls are immeasurably more understanding than boys, I know. Still, for the minute, though she'd heard them before, Liz found my sentiments abominable. I went on with my kicking, which she might have found really irritating, I can't think why. A chap should be free to kick a stone if he likes it.

"History," I said, "has landed us in a valley that's all dry bones. That's what they've taught us, growing up. A derelict car dump, the sign of the modern city. And they expect us to fight to keep it derelict. Imagine the wraiths and scarecrows rising out of it, and shouting victory. Brandishing some rawl plug they might have salvaged. Strippers they are. And they'll be stripped and left for dead. Liz, we should be so happy at seventeen!"

"But you make it so difficult. You seem determined not to be. I go over like a litany all the things I care about, only there's too many, and you make me so exasperated."

"But you will let me talk to you, Liz, won't you?" I was full of alarm. "There's so few people to talk to, and so little to say. I can't ever seem to come on anybody. Except Limp, and you, and I'm worried about him, Liz. He seems unfastened in some way. Moving. Moving as if he must be independent, take on the world by himself."

"Oh, dear."

"Does he really need to be as lonely as that?"

"No, oh, no," said Liz. "Please, we've got to share. To share our lives. It's desperately necessary," Liz said.

49

9

For a bit Robin and John wouldn't even speak to me. And when they spoke to each other, it had to be in a low tone, as though I were on my deathbed, for goodness' sake!

Dad noticed.

"What's up? What's up, Man Friday?"

"All my friends — " I said.

"Look here, that's the least of it. They're just a luxury of the past. Wheels and engines have canceled them out. They're as expendable as pennies. It isn't possible any longer to live with other people. The faster we get, the more centrifugal."

Dad sure hammered it home. Appalling words every one, and all in the dictionary. It was Dad that made me wonder whether barbarism was old or new, and then I began to wonder whether it was perhaps a state of mind. Clean contrary to Liz he was. They were the quiet poles, or at least one of them was quiet, and I was their equator.

About the end of the week when we'd been sacked,

I chanced on John and he said, "Well, ass-face, what ya suppose ya gonna do now?"

John was doing Med. II, and he was home early that afternoon and ran into me in the house, where he obviously thought I shouldn't have been.

"Dunno," I said. "It's only a few months to the exams. I can swot it all up at home. We've been through the syllabus. I'll just about do it as well at home as at school. Some ways maybe better, even."

Played it cool. It was a moderate speech and went on, to show that I took pains with his own attitude, whatever it might be.

"Don't come that bull's twang," said he. So my words were wasted as yet; he was still very peeved. All his mates were flogging our poster paint to death.

"Take the brain boxes," he said. "They just close down when I show up. So I know what they've been magging about, see? But, then, the hobbyhorses, they're the end. They clap you on the shoulder and crack some fool jest and take as much credit as though they'd done the whole damn thing themselves."

"I know the type. I know the type, John. Vicarious bully-boys. You don't need to worry about them."

"No, but when I'm feeling what adventurous hypocrites they all are, I can't think of any answers, can I? They think I'm gonna boast about it, too."

"Why don't you just mutter 'punk' and walk away?"

"Might try it," he said, gloomily, "but it's all your fault. You're mad. And why should I crap off my pals for you?"

John was sour and sore, sore as if we'd gone and painted our notice on his bottom — or boils maybe,

51

that'd have been sorer there? But it irritated us both. There wasn't any good talking, for we cordially understood each other already.

The best thing would have been to spar and fight, like kids again, but I knew, if there was any fight over it, that I was underneath with no right to win. Mum had faded into the kitchen for the past few days and Dad could hardly risk the slightest conversation with her. To me she was extra kind, very often, and it made me feel terrible. Still, I wasn't going to have John grizzling and virtuous while I turned the other cheek and gave him good advice forever.

"All bull's twang," he said. "You can't live here all day, man, it's impossible. It's Dad's territory and he roams all over it all day, reciting things to himself. You'll be getting yourself expelled from this place next— "

"Look here, John — "

" — getting in the way of his work, or — "

"Wish I could get out of yours."

"None of your sauce. At least I have work, and what excuse have you for living?" And he made to strike me a blow on the chest and another higher up.

But I lifted my arm as he hit me, and he knocked it up, and my finger caught in his specs, and they fell, and one of the lenses broke. He swore pretty trenchantly, and I was cursing my fate. Why the hell did I have to meet him tramping our house? There's all the room you need in Australia till you get inside a house. The whole house came running. Everybody hears everything. That's why the sentry boxes are still out there in the yards.

I was so mortified. But what about the day when the Mixmaster bowl went flying? Mum did that. Everybody was cool then. Also the jam boiled over and we all had to hear why it stuck to the roof instead of the floor. James Watt got the blame for that one. It's just that nobody seems to anticipate the things I do.

One day I went out to have a leak in the outside lav, which we kept mainly for the prestige of two toilets. And I was just whistling away and bothering nobody, just whistling about my own business. And when I dropped the seat the whole contraption fell to bits. You think I'm exaggerating? Well, I'm not. It fell, like Stalingrad. And it brought them all running again.

Luckily when I broke John's specs Robin was still at work. But Mum's only a schoolteacher and doesn't work too long.

"Ian, Ian — "

"Makes me absolutely furious."

"Really, Ian, I'll have to take you to the doctor to get some pills."

"Get some for me while you're at it. Mad? I can't stand much more of this."

"Why can't you — "

"I'll have to go on sedation right away. Sure you haven't got a tail inside your pants like a bloody kangaroo? Big as you are, I'll take such a swipe at you — "

"How ever did it happen, Ian?"

"Yes, how *did* it happen? Can't leave you alone for five minutes but everything disintegrates. Been the same ever since you were a kid."

"I was only passing through the lounge room — "

"Lounge room? Where's that?"

53

"I forgot, Dad," I said.

Hell, a chap could never fall into one kind of trouble in our house. Dad had this terrible set against lounge rooms and driveways and hallways. Sheer excuses, he called them.

"All these to-hell-shaped lounges. Don't tell me we've got to admit they're rooms as well."

"Oh, what does it matter? With John's glasses broken. And the bill we'll get. And how can he study? And we've heard it all before."

"It's not extirpated, though. He just said — "

But Mum refused to listen. "Ian," she said, "didn't I tell you when you took the pile off the carpet with that golf club — "

"Golf club! Don't give him that, for Pete's sake. With only his bare hands he's a lurking nuclear bomb. No wonder they threw him out, no — "

"That's nothing to do with it, and you promised. No casting that up, please. We don't cast up to you. And you promised me."

Mum was pretty firm and full of energy. They were looking straight at each other. Thought we might have had some of Dad's glad perennial youth for a minute. Mum sometimes charged Dad with having a ukelele once, and it gave Dad hell to hear it. But this wasn't about a ukelele; and Dad slid out of it.

"Maybe I did promise, maybe I did," he said. "But I didn't reckon on this now, did I? There's nothing in breaking promises if he's going around breaking everything in his reach!"

But Mum held on to her advantage. "Like father, like son. You know very well what I mean." Mum's proverbs were inclined to be a bit more shopworn than Dad's, but she sold him that one.

John had been trying to make himself heard, to take some of the blame. Funny how they'd never thought of blaming him. He said he'd started it. He wasn't a bad chap for a brother, if only to punch now and then.

But Mum said, "If you'd brought up these boys properly, none of this would ever have happened. But that's what's lacking in this house."

"I knew it, I knew it. I knew how it would turn out. I knew I'd have knocked the blasted things off."

"It's the lead their father should have given them. It isn't there. At all. And don't try to tell me it is."

Dad was showing signs of making off, but he made one more disastrous speech of it. He'd recovered some of his exasperation. It was something they did for each other.

"Go on, go on. I apologize. Went through the lounge on horseback like Absalom, and whisked John's specs in my spurs."

"Don't be silly. Please. You're about the place far too much. Filling it full of bad language all day. Why can't you go out and work like decent men?"

"But I think I will, God damn it, think I will. Anything's better than being in range."

Dad hopped off to his den and charged about. But that wasn't Mum's way. She kept it, turned it into dyspepsia. But if Dad had stayed in his den, all his work would have been ruined. Finally Mum went off to her bedroom and slammed the door. I knew she would be sobbing. So did Dad. And now there was the rage of regret to bear. We kept mooning about and watching Mum's door and wondering whether you could be sorry about something you had so totally caused, and so unnecessary.

"Can't you even make a cup of tea?" Dad said, once. "Not that anybody'll drink it."

After a bit I thought I might go down the bush with the dog and have a chat with Andy, who lived in a shack there, and find out whether he found life peaceful. But then I thought that first of all I might try speaking to Mr. Waterhouse. I had an idea how he could help me in my troubles, so I phoned him from a call box at the bus terminus. He was most understanding. Most.

What made me think of him was his being a contractor, in a big way. He might have a job that I could do till everybody got used to me being finished with school. And I wanted to come to Mum at the end of the week and give her all my dough, and maybe pat her hand and squeeze it on all the crinkly dollar bills.

I just said at once, "Mr. Waterhouse?"

He said, "Yes, who's speaking, please?"

"I just wondered if you'd have a job I could do, Mr. Waterhouse, wheeling bricks or anything? It's Ian Guthrie."

His voice changed then. He was quite pleased to speak to me. I could tell.

"Oh, it's you, Ian. I thought I'd be seeing you around our place. But you haven't shown up."

I hadn't gone anywhere very much.

"Perce is expecting you. How are you? What can I do for you?"

"D'you think there's any job I could do for a month or so, Mr. Waterhouse? Till I know where I am?"

"How about pushing a pneumatic drill, for instance?"

"Fine. Can I start tomorrow?"

He'd been sounding me out, half joking. But I wasn't.

"Easy, easy on it. We'll see. Come around anyway and I'll fix you with something all right. Your folks agreeable?"

"Oh, they're agreeable."

"Sure now?"

"Well, Mr. Waterhouse, they're a bit stunned and all that, but they know it'd be a good thing I weren't just loafing at home. Everybody beefing, you know? It's how I came to ring you, in fact."

"I know how it is," he said.

He was very sympathetic.

When I got away from the phone I breathed with relief and hoped it would already have secretly eased Mum's sobbing. I thought I'd be able to keep Mr. Waterhouse to it. I'd have liked to bespeak a jackhammer for Limp, too, but he mightn't have wanted it. You can't press every kind of opportunity on your friends.

It worked out, though, for me. On Monday I was three floors up on a big old building they were taking down. Clouds of dust, danger money and all, $40 a week. I told him I wanted to give it all to Mum and that finished him. He made me promise to be extra careful, said I was working now. And I was, I was careful. I'm not always a fool.

57

10

___

MUM WOULDN'T KEEP my first week's pay, but only half of it. Even then she gave me it back, in kind. Shirts and things. After that she took $10 and left me the rest. They feel they're robbing you, I don't know how it is. I suppose it's this reversing of the habit of a lifetime, like finding yourself dead or in the army. Which must be a bit of a shocker. Anyway, it made a heck of a difference at home.

I presented it all to Mum the moment I got in. Dad stood in the kitchen and watched me count it into her hand. He was holding out his hand, too, but it stayed empty. He even put it behind his back when I flourished five dollars his way. There were only the three of us, and we all said, " — Twenty-five, thirty, thirty-five, forty," and smiled and cheered and looked as if we'd never seen that much money before.

They were acting like I'd gone back to being a baby, when everything I did was for astonishment. It hardly needs explaining, but it was fun. Why couldn't it always be like that?

But Dad also said, "Of course, we haven't changed our minds about that offer I made you."

"O.K., Dad, O.K., I'm thinking about that."

It introduced a sour note at once, as Dad was inclined to do. It never seemed to matter to him that there was a time for everything. After all, working by himself, he'd lost the habit of any discipline toward other people. He just blurted things out at them when it occurred to him, take it or leave it. As for Dad, he could walk away and live in his own spirit. He was sufficient to himself, and thought the world would be a better place if everybody else was, too. But it wouldn't, would it?

I was puzzled about this, because I could see that in some ways my very best friends — Limp and Liz — tended to be a bit like him. Nothing swerved them. The difference was that Dad marched on his way in spite of anything, elected to believe that nothing else was there. But Limp and Liz weren't that way at all, especially Liz. She thought life was for sharing, and it made me spy the woman in her. Limp and Liz could think about a matter, and adjust. And so they were beginning to see how difficult a process this was, if you did it conscientiously. And if you did it conscientiously, that sure meant that you did it by yourself and on nobody else's say-so. But you couldn't empty the world to Dad's extent. If you got rid of what you didn't like, it was very apt to take what you liked along with it.

Of course, at the time I did know there was sense in Dad's remark. I'm not accusing him of lack of sense, I hope. Everything is so complicated, and if you want to tease it out it takes hours. And we certainly should tease it out. So as to earn judgment, and short methods of judgment. It really makes for speed and soundness, both. Young folk should think around and around — and some of them still do. That's not a guess. I know. There's seriousness in the young. They're not solemn, that's all. And they shouldn't be.

Well, you see, Dad had made this proposition.

"All right," he said, "I'll help Limp with his English, and this is how. You're to be in the class as well. You too will study for the Higher School Certificate, and the class and the study will go to a regular plan, which will be agreed on before I saddle my blackboard and chalk. Sworn to before I spit a syllable. Else it's no go," Dad said, "no go at all."

But hadn't I had enough of schools and exams? I wanted to get some profit out of being expelled from school. The hell with being expelled and still doing lessons and homework. Stuff that. That would be the worst of both worlds.

And I made this clear to him.

Dad walked away. Just shrugged it off. "That's it then," he said.

So when I was counting the money into Mum's hand, he would have been thinking that here was another step away from order and matriculation and the insurance that it was, for any man's life. That the encouragement of a little money would seduce me farther away. Maybe it was a proper time to speak, after all?

I thought I'd better go and see Limp.

I must have been secretly hoping that Limp would take Dad's offer and necessitate my taking it, too, without the bother of any more decision on my part. I could shove along with Limp at the one elbow and Dad at the other. It was a way I liked to proceed. And even to have Liz kicking me up the tail, so long as I could look back and see her doing it, and dodge. Girls concentrate their faces and often put out their tongues and always look comical when they try kicking you in the tail. And they always kick too high. So that you can sometimes catch their leg. If you're not being frog-marched by the elbows, that is.

There was also something I thought on to please Limp's mum, and I'm not embarrassed about it. When I got to their house, I said good evening and hoped I wasn't disturbing them. I put my closed hands on the table and repeated, slowly,

> *"Neevie, neevie, nick-nack,*
> *Which hand will you tak?"*

They knew the game, and we'd played it before — kids' stuff.

So Limp's mum screwed up her face and laughed and took the right hand. It was one of the five-dollar notes from my first pay. Actually, I had another in the other hand, which I shoved rapidly in my pocket.

It's what I did, and I know it's boasting, but I wanted to do it. I still had a devil of a job getting them to take it. Maybe it was an invasion of their independence. Maybe I should have said I was sorry in some other way, but I couldn't think of any. Limp's mum had been kind to me for years, and I couldn't I be kind to her for one evening at least?

But Limp, to my surprise, wouldn't take on Dad's proposition either.

"I've been thinking about it since you said. And not this year."

"But Limp, you're nineteen and it could be your last chance. Don't be ridiculous, man."

"Not this year, last chance or not. Game of chess?" he said.

So we had a game of chess and I went on thinking about the mistake he was making and I lost miserably. But that was nothing. He always played me with one of his castles off the board. He was teaching me chess, and it's a matchless game. Gets you so absorbed. It's so matchless that you can finish up like Dad, single-handed, with nothing to your life but chess. So I don't play at all now.

It was late when I got home, so on Saturday at breakfast I recklessly told Dad that Limp said thanks, of course, but wasn't going on with the H.S.C. Dad took it on his marmalade, concentrated on the table-cloth, gnawed at his toast, finally grunted sideways in good English and looked out at the garden. But Mum said, "Robin and I both think Ian should sit the H.S.C., whatever else he does."

"It's plenty by itself," said Robin severely.

And John was saying, making no effort to catch up, "Sure. So do I."

He put his energy into it, scrum down. I suppose he was considering how you sit the H.S.C., usually, on zero dollars a week, which was his own income.

I saw my mistake by then. Dad didn't really need to say anything if he felt like a rest. But, "Yes," he said, "a hobo's always a better hobo for being well qualified. What do you say, son?"

"Oh," I said, "I don't mean to be a hobo."

I could see how it was going. It was too early in the morning to fend the truth off. But I was playing for time, preserving my liberty as long as I could. You'd need an unsleeping impudence to face my family. Generally, they weren't all on one side, and here, not only that, but they were on my side as well. I was secretly thrilled to bits, and on Saturday, at breakfast time.

"What do you mean to be then?" Robin said. Or, rather, it was almost a triumphant shout.

It wasn't a thing I'd ever given a thought to, but Mum chipped in and saved me from any sudden decision that might have marred me for life.

"It's so ironical. There's a happy-go-lucky knack. He's a lucky boy, yet everything seems to happen to him at the worst possible time. Yes, he must sit his exams, and put his back into it. He hasn't been studying."

"I don't know," Dad said. "Writing all day long with this damn big pneumatic pencil. It's good practice. If he could only take it into the exam hall . . ."

"Oh, no more of it," Mum said. "I get rather tired of you. Let's have a sensible suggestion and not a curly one, please."

"How many weeks to the exams?" Dad said.

"About two months," I said. I knew exactly. "But I don't think I could do it. You know how it is with a pneumatic drill. Drives everything out of your head. Like ghosts from an enchanter fleeing."

"Humph," Dad said. "That settles it. English, dead cert. History, should fluke it. French? He's always liked languages, you know, Mum. Might do Latin even better than French, for all I know. But the mathematics, there's the rub."

"I couldn't do the mathematics in a month of Sundays. That's why I don't want to try it. Needs constant practice, too."

"John can't help you," Dad said, glumly. "He's enough on his plate."

"Oh," John groaned, "maybe — "

He took so long to say "oh" that Robin just wouldn't wait.

"Dad," she said, "he needs taking by the seat of the pants, that's all he needs. I've seen him at his books, and he wants to sit it. He's not all fool, really. Surely he isn't going to be allowed to slope out of this as usual?"

She sounded disgusted, but not entirely, either. Of course, maybe there was something about the Guthries that made them go for lost causes, like Oxford, but it was something I hadn't ever noticed in Robin. She was interested. She was right about my wanting to sit it, too. Gee, I thought, it's good when your big sister bothers a bit about you.

"It's the maths, Robin," I said. "I like all the others, could just about have a whack at them. But not the maths. And then I couldn't matriculate, so what's the use?"

"If you'd only . . ." said Mum, and her voice died away and she looked desperate.

"If he'd only had the sense he was born with," Dad said, "and stayed on at school. Far better than forty dollars a week."

"There's one thing for it," Robin said, sitting up with a bounce on the front of her chair, raising her finger, knitting her brows like a schoolmarm. "It's quite easy to see. You've got to sit it. Even if you stop at four subjects, you can do the other one in February. Keep you out of mischief for the summer." She smiled.

"Oh, well, look here, chaps," I said, "since you're all so interested, and to give Limp a lead, I'll have a go. Don't rouse on me if I don't manage too well — "

Everybody was pleased. "Well done, Robin," Mum said. "This is a happy day."

"But it takes me longer than two months, as a rule," I said, "to do the impossible."

Dad revived at that. "Not you," he said. "Give you about five minutes, that's all you need. You can take yourself down to my den three or four evenings a week, and I'll be your man-midwife."

Mum was laughing at most of that. She seemed pleased with Dad, and amused at his offer. "A hair of the dog that — oh!" she said.

I don't suppose you would ever have worked a pneumatic drill, would you? There's nothing to it, but you wouldn't need to be a nervous cove, that's all. It's like a motor mower, only worse. Shakes you up all around the seating of your ribs. I used to feel it worst at night when I lay down. It's one of those jobs where you can sow the wind and reap the whirlwind. I used to have to sit up in bed, till the hurly-burly inside me had died down and the witches had gone looking for Macbeth. It might have been flatulence, but I don't think so. More like palpitation, but I didn't ever inquire and I didn't tell Mum at all. If I didn't bolt my dinner when I was tired, I could easily avoid it, and I wasn't going to do it for long, anyway. Just till I had enough money saved up, and Mr. Waterhouse didn't always need me to knock places down for him.

There was this guy at work who had an old Morris pre-war, a tourer, the sort of thing that's handy for slinging papers around from. One hundred bucks he wanted for it. Advertised it on his windscreen all the time. $100 (FULL PRICE), brackets and all. They're an eight-horsepower job, as you know, and I've never heard of anybody having much trouble with them.

I'm pretty handy with cars. It's a thing you get nowadays as you grow up, like your voice breaking. And girls expect it. And my brother John's got a good husky baritone for cars as well, and can keep it up, long after my suggestions have gone pretty operatic: coloratura, anyway.

I said John could have the use of this bomb if I bought it, provided he helped me put it right and keep it right. It might need a few things done, I said. Would he come and look it over for me? I was grave and tactful as an estate agent.

"Oh," he said, "if it's running about — I haven't the time. All you'll want is enough steam to get the thing home, and whenever Mum sees it you won't be needing the engine anymore. It'll stack up in the yard whether the pistons work or not."

Brilliant John was about it. He was never really benign about my $40 a week. But I had to be patient with him since my whole capital was involved.

"One hundred bucks he's asking."

"Offer him eighty. You'll soon see whether he's on the level. I know a bloke got that model for only sixty bucks. Runs like a beaut, too."

I didn't know how I'd see he was on the level, but I did as John said.

"Give you eighty for that bus," I said, next day at smoko.

"On the nail?" he said.

"Next payday."

"It's a deal," he said, and it was then I felt the need of what John said. How could he be on the level? He had $100 on his flaming windscreen. I never thought he'd just accept like that at once. Must be something phony. Maybe I was a mug. What the hell *did* I know about cars, anyway?

And Mum and Dad didn't know a thing about it at all. I was that worried I very nearly put the drill through my damn left foot.

"What d'ya think old Giles's bus is worth?" I said to another old codger.

"Scrap heap, I'd say. You want to watch old Giles."

It wasn't exactly cheering. But when he knew I was buying it he said just the opposite. "You'll be right," he said. "Old Giles wouldn't do the dirty on one of his mates."

"But you just said — "

"Forget it. Slinging off, old sport, slinging off. You don't want to pay no heed. Tell you what, I'll have a yarn with the foreman about it. He knows all the dope."

He did, too. He had a yarn with the foreman about it. There were some very decent guys in that mob. Does you good to meet up with them.

The foreman came over and spoke about it himself. It was smashing of him.

"You know very damn much about cars, young 'un?"

"Not much."

"Thought not," he said. "You know very damn much about Giles?"

"No," I said. I was tired of saying "not much."

"Thought not," he said. "You'll have heard of goannas, though? Blue-tongues?"

Big blue-tongues. Who hasn't? And they'll say as much to you as anybody you happen to meet. Anybody at all elderly. I began to think I'd as soon hear the old drill talking. This foreman took his job like a Roman senator — addressing me up the rhetorical forum.

So I said, "Yes, I'm quite friendly with one. Lives in the same place as I do — Seven Carluke Street."

"Don't come the crap," he said. "Cos I'm tellin' you Giles ain't got no more in 'is 'ead 'n a bleedin' goanna. An' 'e's cold-blooded like they are, as well. I been workin' along o' Giles for longer 'n you been breathin', an' I know. You can take it from me, son. Cut 'is thumb oncet, deep, did old Giles, an' it didn' even bleed. 'Ow come, Giles? I says an' 'e says, George, 'e says, my great-grandfather 'e was a bleedin' goanna, I reckon. One as escaped the abos' bloody cook pot. No bull! Fourth-generation Australian, Giles 'e says, that's me. No sense in 'is 'ead, an' no bleedin' blood in 'is bleedin' veins, that's Giles."

You'll hear guys shooting the bull about how

they're fourth-generation Australians and I calculate it's because the convicts were all free by then, counting backward. It exonerates them to go back only to 1860 or so.

"Ah, well," the foreman said, "oncet you've 'ad the valves ground, an' new piston rings, an' the carburettor replaced, an' all Marge Giles's sewing machine parts took out an' returned to 'er, I reckon you'll maybe get yer money's worth out'n old Giles's bus yet, I shouldn't wonder. As for the diff," he said, "you won't 'ave to worry none about that. Guess it must 'ave fell off long ago. Ah, well," he said, "what's done's done. No good bein' a bloody pessimist about it, is there? An' maybe makin' you anxious, or castin' a cuppla teeth. But next time," he said, "come to me quick-smart afore ya do anything an' then maybe I'll be able to 'elp youse wiv a bit o' sound advice."

"I'll do that, thanks," I said.

"You'll be right, young 'un. Right as Bob Menzies, you will, an' it's far too right for me."

He lifted his hat, wiped a bit of sweat with his forearm, rolled a cigarette. It was tattooed all over — his forearm, that is.

"If it ever comes to pass as 'is grandfather was a goanna, as 'e said, then 'e's a credit to the species, old Giles is. You could put yer shorts on Giles an' still have 'em after."

It was a bit of comfort, I suppose, and I didn't know them well enough to go back on my word. I just had to buy that bomb on payday. And I did. To hear the foreman talk, I knew there must be something corny, but I reckoned it was his conversation.

69

11

"STAB ME, LIZ, d'you know what he's going to do? He's going to volunteer."

"Who?" said Liz.

"Limp," I said. "D'you mind if I come around and talk to you about it?" We were on the phone.

"All right," said Liz. "What's the time? Oh, ten past five. You'll have to be gone when Dad gets back, that's all."

"What time's he back?"

"Ten past six."

"Oh, easy, easy. We'll finish the war by that time, Liz, just about. I'll be right there."

But when I got there I had to do some horsing with Rod, didn't think I'd ever get a private word with Liz at all. She had to give him a hint and between brothers and sisters hints have to be extremely uproarious to take effect. Which this hint couldn't be before me. Liz was so peeved at the predicament she was in that she nipped away to her bedroom.

"Look here," I said to Rod, "piss off, will you?" And grieved him.

"You come to see me," he said, "and tell me to piss off?"

"No," I said, "I didn't come to see you. I came to see Liz."

"Oh," he said, "it's that way. Snaking my sister, are you? Does she know?"

"Yes," I said. "No," I said. "That's just the trouble," I said. "Oh, look here, Rod — "

"Look here, you idiot, what's it all about?"

"I mean, Rod, you think I've come like a jolly thriving wooer and Liz knows you'll think that and she's gone for fear of it and it's not that at all. I've something to discuss with her, *see?* You big oaf."

"Oh," he said, "I don't see. But I know when I'm not wanted. So long," he said, and left me standing on the verandah. And he hammered on Liz's door as he passed.

"Liz!" he shouted. "Richard the Third!"

Which I must say was very clever of Rod, for he was totally incapable of the unexpected, I would have thought. But then Pansy had been drilling that phrase into us all the year. It made me remember how Rod was still at school. He sank into his usual lethargy very soon after, though; for he started up the mower and went back and forth on the lawn in front of us, upbraiding me with his nonchalance, braying out bursts of the latest hit tunes, while the night was falling around about him and the starlings were fussing in Mutch's camellia trees.

It might have been ten to six, and Liz had to get something off her chest even then.

"There's something about you," Liz said, "whenever you get with people, that you underrate. You always have to be horsing about with them. You always have to flatter them by being an even greater ass than you think they are. I know my brother isn't very bright," Liz said. She was in the same school year and fourteen months younger than Rod. "But the way you have to keep on insulting him with peanuts, with sheer stupidities, isn't funny. I notice it with Perce, I notice it with Sue, and your sister, and even John, and your mum, and there's never an end to it. Headmaster, chairman, you scatter them all, because you despise them. Or so you think, but it's yourself you scatter. Wish you'd grow up. Not be so annoying."

She stopped fast, biting her words back, and I began to admire the music of Rod's mower, even. I picked at my chair.

"Gee whiz," I said, "to hear you talk, Liz, you'd think we were married already."

"Oh, who would marry you?" she exclaimed, a bit quickly, I thought. I just thought it might have occurred to her, since she came in quickly then, that's all, and it revived me. And chivalrously I changed the subject.

"About Limp," I said.

She was suddenly quite eager to speak about him. Girls are great fun, far better than Rod with or without his mower, or me to horse about with him. I love them far better.

"He mightn't be picked out," Liz said. "It's too early to worry yet."

"You think so? Well, he has to register next week, and he's dead against being chucked into the army on a lottery, because of a bad war, which we wouldn't be in at all if America weren't in it, or if America could have found better friends, for that matter. Bigger ones, like France or Britain."

Liz had the sensible answer. "Communism. It's got to be stopped. It's ugly and brutal. It pays no heed to any single person. Naked power and that's all. We didn't stop it in Tibet, for instance. Or the Baltic states. Or even Hungary. We've got to choose possible places, and possible ways. It spreads by war. Force is its only element."

Gee, though, I thought, got to be careful, Liz is beginning to look like Queen Victoria. This won't do.

"You said he was going to volunteer?" Liz said, more practical.

"He thinks he should go down and say to them: 'I don't want to be dragooned, I'll volunteer for two years.' Reckons he'll feel better about it if he offers. As you might offer Mum to clean the bath, when you see it coming. It's not a thing you ever *want* to do," I said.

"I see," Liz said. "But they won't have him that way."

"Why, Liz?"

"Because they've got him the other way. Or somebody else."

"Yes, it's like picking strawberries. You just take the ones you fancy. Say, Liz, do you think they've any right to appropriate twenty-year-olds? How would you feel if they came along and said, 'Hey, you, Liz, we're taking your life and body. Come along with us for two years'? For that's what they're doing to young men. And only some young men, a very few young men. They say it's a fair go."

Liz looked bleak, sighed, banged her thighs in the dusk. "It's after six," she said.

"All right, I'll go. Liz, I've got a proposal to make. Oh, not that kind of proposal."

"I wasn't thinking of that."

"Oh, yes you were, Liz, you know you were. But what I mean — "

"Just thought you were being silly. Your usual silly self," Liz said, vexed, but managing to smile.

" — is this. It's this I mean. Supposing a boy and girl, like us, were to stop people in the street among the shops and ask them what they thought of the present conscription setup?"

"Don't want to. Why us?"

"Because we're the ones affected. Would you do it on Saturday for an hour? What do you think they'd say?"

"They wouldn't be interested."

"But shall we try?"

Liz shrugged. She wasn't keen. Admittedly, for any public action, you had to be tough as the name of Pankhurst. And married, preferably. It's a protection.

"You just don't want to be seen with me, Liz, that's what?"

"All right," she said, "I'll come. But only for half an hour. Oh, gosh," Liz cried, "can I bring Sue? It's like soliciting. I don't think so. Don't think I'll come."

I was going down the steps, and off.

"See you Saturday. It's on. Just you. Why, Liz, it's

74

worth finding out about. Hell, Liz, to be conscripted's an important matter for a boy! To be robbed of himself. So coolly. By chance."

Then at the foot of the steps I looked up and appealed for Liz's smile. And she gave it to me. She drew back her hair and put both hands on the verandah rail and sprang on it and was young and waved as she turned to the house.

12

"GOD SHAKE IT," Dad said, "don't we ever get any peace?"

The dog was barking and there would be a boy friend any minute. Quite recently a bomb had exploded in the street. It was the evening after my assignation with Liz.

Dad was always threatening to draw the bow of Ulysses. He'd make short work, he said, of those sons of wooers.

"Why sons of wooers?" asked John.

I was wondering, too. I was interested in metaphor. But he was off. It infuriated Dad to stay and have his health inquired into. "Can't keep my house to myself or my daughter to myself," he said, "but I'm damned if I'll share my health with them." Real possessive Dad was. "After a month or two," he said, "and from then on for the rest of their lives, it won't occur to them that I'm healthy."

Robin had learned to take it all with a sharp, haughty silence, but it made Mum mad. She'd done her best to persuade Dad that Robin's boy friends had to come to the house. The trouble was, Dad quite agreed with her. They still gave him these jack-in-the box feelings, nevertheless. Dad reckoned the also-rans weren't worth it. When the time came to cheer the winner, he'd be there. It's a great length to go with puritanism, and self-sufficiency. It's a ferocious attitude to life.

John beetled off, too, but he called it politeness. "Hell," he said, "you wouldn't suppose anybody's coming just for the love of you, would ya?"

But I thought maybe somebody should give a kind of token assurance that we all lived in our house. Dennis Morney came in, and I began to regret it.

"Howdy, Junior," he said.

If there's one thing I hate it's being called Junior, especially by dopes.

"Heard this one? You may be a bright spark, but you're still no Champion." It's the name of a Goddamned sparkplug, for heaven's sake.

"If I were you, Dennis," I said, "I wouldn't go in for the used-joke trade."

"I don't quite get you, but I suppose it's good advice. And how's Robin?"

He tried freezing me off, and tackling Robin in the third person. Robin was blasted annoyed, and he could have seen it without asking. Just before I left, I thought I might try him with our project for Saturday.

"What's your opinion on the National Service Act, Dennis?"

"What's the National Service Act?" said he, bursting with repartee.

So I left them, and Robin shouted, "Good riddance!"

Morney by himself was enough of a strain on Robin's temper. I knew he was just wasting his time, but you can't tell a chap that. Hurts his ego.

Dad wasn't even painting when I got there. He was shifting everything about in a plague of nervous energy.

"I think we'd better do some work for the H.S.C., don't you think? As an extra, since I can't settle my mind? Let's give our attention to this villanelle, for instance. Sit down and sit up."

Dad took the coaching in his stride. Often he even seemed to know what he was talking about — when it came to English, e.g. There were surprising things that Dad was a genius at and we had some hilarious sessions. I think he liked the sudden upsurge of company, and aim. Mum said it was this hair of the dog that bit him. I never could tell just what I was in for. I mean,

What the hell
Was a villanelle?

"You do right to ask," Dad said. "And just notice that it's a rhetorical question very nearly like 'Can any good come out of Nazareth?' Springs straight out of speech. Don't ever be so crappy as to think that figures of speech are figures of poetry. They're figures . . . of speech, see?"

I said I wouldn't be so crappy. "But this villanelle?" I said.

"Poetry," said Dad, "is the most ordinary thing in the world. You mustn't get the idea it's something up there in the sky. I'll show you. I've written this villanelle and a villanelle's the most delicate thing in the world. Nineteen lines to say your say, and to say it with a great deal of artistic grace, and not lose sight of the gutter altogether. For it's got to be about what happens now and the gutter's practically all we've got."

Dad was turning this big whiteboard around on the easel. Now that he was finished preparing the class, he set it longwise on its pins, and nervously seized a pointer. The whole thing was in neat black print, must have taken him hours. It surprised me continually how Dad took so much pains with what was beautiful. Then I read this title: *On Seeing a Little Dung in the Road.*

"Stap me," I said.

Villanelle; On Seeing a Little Dung in the Road

> *These days a man might well*
> *stop at a little dung in the road*
> *and wonder how the hell*
>
> *such ancientry befell,*
> *leaping alive and young in the road*
> *and yet so medieval.*
>
> *I seem to see the ruined pile*
> *a heap of chivalry flung in the road:*
> *glimpses of the feudal*
>
> *make my days less technical.*
> *Other ages come in the road*
> *on foot, with peal of bell.*
>
> *Sewers of civil petrol and oil*
> *indecently go bung in the road.*
> *I'd have the world go animal*

rather than be living still
this midden of the mechanical
that has us stunk and stung, by God,
far worse than any dung in the road.

"Wrote it myself," Dad said. "It's a raw villanelle. I can't help, somehow, but burst through the rules. If you're fit, I'll show you its points. The poem's neat; and contradictory; more serious than its tone; about the common world; two rhymes interlacing, see; breaking its thought at the thirteenth line in this one; keeping you in mind of the whole long Western tradition, and the revolution in technology and exhaust pipes, and the religiousness of life and poetic form. Now what's Morney saying tonight?"

It was his way of saying gently that the lesson was done. Abrupt and embarrassed Dad was, when he bared his mind to a class of one. It was a pity, he said, that Limp wasn't having any, for it would have halved Dad's personal responsibility. But what the hell could he mean?

13

"OH, MORNEY! This Morney chap," I said to Dad, "he
thinks the National Service Act's only a witty pastime.
What do you think about it?"

"I can't think of it with patience. It darkens my life,"
Dad said. He stopped his tidying up. "You see, I've two
sons. Though one of them escaped. A snare of the
fowler," Dad said.

"Can't anything be done about it?"

"Not here. It's a job for an opposition. Democracies
have declined. A country's suffering pretty good
government when there's two parties, and only two,
and they're disputing the rule. They keep each other
to it. Gladstone and Disraeli, Pitt and Fox, God and
the Devil. They keep each other up to the mark. But
there's one thing more," Dad said.

"And what's that, Dad?"

"They need an electorate that can appreciate them.
Or at least understand. To debate great matters needs
very attentive, nervous, responsible listeners. Rhetoric's
all right in the racket of the seashore, but good argument isn't."

"And . . . universal suffrage, aren't you for it?"

Dad shook his head sadly. "I ought to be, oughtn't I? But I'm not. There's too much of the demagogue, too much of the leader, too much of the image. He's halfway to being a dictator, a tyrant, fixing what will serve. And he's paper-thin. You can see underneath to how ordinary he is. That's the party leader, a carpet-bagger if ever there was. No, men will have their heroes still, but they won't spring out of the vote. No Sir Robert Peels that way."

"Was he a hero?"

"Yes," Dad said. "He didn't fix. Rose above party. And himself. Events have still to educate this country. There are no public questions, except about pub-closing. Because the public aren't interested in questions, have no great newspapers, don't see themselves involved in great concerns. Except as somebody's buddy. Britain's. Or America's."

"Why don't you do something if you really think all this?"

Dad shrugged and scratched his head. "I wouldn't know where to begin."

"You could turn your gifts that way. You're an artist. Robin says you taught once. Looks as though you've wearied in well-doing, Dad."

"Yes," Dad said. "I had enough of that. But you're right, of course. Take a warning. What'll you do?"

"I can't tell you," I said. "But I'm thinking."

"Then I'm really pleased," said Dad, sighing in a very tired way. "Really pleased. You'll have it hard. And giving up is always so easy. The pursuit of happiness doesn't rest the soul, but it does cancel it out."

"Craps me," I said. "All these bitter shining sayings. I always thought how marvelous it was, bounded in the nutshell of this workshop, thinking everything into axioms like Euclid, but I see it doesn't make any impact on anything. I think I'll do something else when I grow up. Though I like art and poetry and history as well as you do. I'm going."

"You're coming here," Dad said, "to that very end — to pass your exams and do something better. But don't go. You and I will have to talk a bit more. Sit down again," he said.

He wasn't angry, and this surprised me. I'd been so crapped off I meant him to be furious. Had just let fly. Of course I'd heard Robin speak to Dad like that, but then he asked for it, and it was usually with reference to boy friends and all sorts of other folk that Dad was easily convicted of not being interested in. Even the neighbors you can admit to not knowing these days. So Dad just let Robin go it. I think he knew he was hard on her — had no sympathy for girls, Mum said. But tonight he said, "If you're shaping to put the world right, I'd better tell you something. In your defense, if not mine. You can cut me off when you like. You see, I've already protested. And your mum tells me every day that it didn't do a scrap of good, not a scrap."

"I — "

"Just listen," he said. "I came out here to be head of a school, a big school. You won't ask to see my qualifications, will you, but I have them. Within four months a visiting English headmaster came marching into my study to meet me and he was saying, 'Good morning, sir. Well, I see School Councils in Australia don't know their business!' 'No,' I said, 'I can't even appoint my own staff.' 'Intolerable,' he said.

"However, that school was at a very low ebb and they needed me. I took advantage to insist on what I wanted, and I got it. Every bit, though they wanted good cricket pitches rather than good masters. Or buildings, buildings called after them. And they put the school chapel in a corner out of sight of the school. It was for weddings only. And so fighting those things I made the old entrenched councilors my enemies, and the young ones, though they liked to hear me confute their elders, were just shaping to grow like them.

"One day a man applied for a post and said, 'I've done this and this, but a psychiatrist has advised me to get back to teaching. I wondered what the Christian schools would do to help me.' And he looked me straight in the eye across my desk, mildly accusing, knowing what he had a right to expect. He'd had a homosexual affair. I knew very well that with a few kind words, a promise to consult the council on his behalf, or even my own wife, I could get him out at the door. It wouldn't have mattered who I spoke to. Nobody would have had him. But Christian schools, he'd said. And the private schools here call themselves that. And I saw Christ, once, quietly writing in the dust.

"I remember," Dad said, grimly. "I've cause. I'm not dramatizing. *Let him that is without sin among you* . . . And I appointed him. 'If you let me down,' I said, 'it'll be the end of me, too.' He was a skillful teacher. And he didn't let me down. But one of his neighbors did. She phoned the council."

"And did you go, Dad?"

84

"No, but the master did. The council noted, and waited. Suppose I can't blame them for that, not at all. It wasn't wise. But I'm grateful to have done it. He was married. It made his wife happy. And the next week he rang me up and thought I might like to know that the Roman Catholic archbishop had appointed him to teach in a school. I was proud of that."

Dad paused to recover his strength. "I don't like telling you this," he said. "It's too complex. A man's whole nature is in it. That's what vindicates or condemns me, not just the words I blurt out. Besides, you'll think I'm only to be condemned now."

"Oh, no," I said.

"Yes," said Dad. "I know I don't serve for much, so what can my words do?

"Soon a very good master that I'd struggled to get was offered a big scholarship to do a Ph.D. It was the beginning of the year. Of course he took it. I had to get another man in a hurry to teach maths and physics to the best forms. Two men applied, and my fellow headmasters said I was lucky that even two did. One was applying because he'd failed in engineering at university. A nice young man, but that was all he had to offer to our senior boys. The other one had his degree, with distinctions in both mathematics and physics. He had taught for a year. But he was a Roman Catholic. He told me this in his application and he was candid enough to add that at the end of the year he was thinking of going abroad. I phoned the chairman and spoke about him.

" 'But he's a Catholic,' I said, 'so I suppose it's no go.'

" 'You have no alternative,' he said.

" 'I'm seeing him on Saturday, and I invite you to come if you like.'

" 'Oh, no,' he said, 'I'm going into the country, but you see him and if you like him, appoint him and it will be all right.'

" 'We could appoint him on a temporary basis. He seems to want to travel.'

" 'Oh, no, if he's all right just appoint him in the ordinary way.'

"He was an excellent young man. I appointed him, and he began on the Monday. We'd been without a master for some weeks. That Thursday at the end of the council meeting the chairman tabled a unanimous repudiation of the appointment of a Roman Catholic."

Dad cleaned his whiteboard slowly.

"What did you do?"

"I was enraged, as they meant me to be. They hadn't asked my version before they repudiated me. It was me they were repudiating. There were Catholics on the staff already, appointed before I came, and by them. I told them what I thought in high indignation.

" 'And now,' I said, 'I'll go and write my resignation.'

" 'I wish you would,' said the chairman, 'for I've never heard such a pack of lies in all my life and I've no confidence in you whatsoever.' "

I was crushed.

"So you see," Dad said, "I'm not very good at protesting. I wrote my resignation, and left them to choose between me and the chairman. I had no doubt they could do that already, and how they would do it.

That Friday the school carpenter said to his wife, 'Mary, you can catch a thief but you can't catch a liar.'

"Now leave me," he said. "I don't mind what outside people think about me. There was a tremendous fuss. But I don't like putting myself up for retrial by my family. I care about them, and their good opinion, though it may not look like it. Scram, buster."

It was one of Mum's phrases, that.

14

———

WHEN LIZ AND I went out that Saturday, life had become far more serious, what with Dad's story and something else. I'd gone and asked Limp to come with us, and at first Liz was real peeved again.

"You wouldn't let me bring Sue," she said.

"You can't compare Sue with Limp, can you?"

"Oh, can't I? She's equally my friend. I don't despise my friends as you do. You've got this queer idea of weighing people in an intellectual balance all the time, and finding them wanting. I suppose clever people nearly always do. Anyway, I'm not doing that. Cuts you off at the edge of the world. I still can tell you plenty things you're not too clever about. It isn't a bit clever to look down your nose at people."

"Why isn't it, Liz? If they aren't worth much."

"Still, to *under*value them. They're worth more than you think. Because they're people. Sue, for instance, is kind, and quick to understand that way. And if you undervalue people," Liz said, slowly, "you can only end up undervaluing yourself. And serve you right."

"Newton's Third Law again!"

"What's that?"

"Nothing. Is that your only reason?"

"What for?"

"For saying I'll end up undervaluing myself. Because it serves me right?"

"No, but because you're a person, too. Silly boy, you can't escape the human race. And shouldn't want to. Underrate everybody, and you'll be as poor a creature as all the rest. Even if you're hopelessly arrogant. Nobody will value you for that. The arrogant man, always, is priding himself on something he's not. And he knows he's not, that's his misery. That's why he exacts every ounce of subordination. You can see it in teachers."

"Well, Liz," I said, "don't give me arrogance. I know one or two arrogant ba —— chaps. Footballers, masters — and they're poorly human. They've got a tin perfection to them. I mean, they try to confine the world to the thing they're good at and the folk that think they're good at it. Exclusives, all of them. Arrogant footballers'll turn up their noses at pictures, poetry, music, good manners, the lot. They're always good players, and here it has come and blinded them. I like football myself," I said. "And it lets you know about people. They're unguarded out of their own clothes, surrendered to the game."

"Are we going for Limp, or aren't we?"

Liz had the trace of a smile lurking on her lips, and loping along beside her of course I saw it. She was trying to purse it away. Actually, I was delighted with myself, squiring Liz in the morning. And she was looking a woman and beautiful. Talking like one, too. But there again she'd opened my eyes on something and she wasn't going to talk about it anymore. It was finished. I had the L plates on, and I was the good learner. That's what she was thinking, I bet.

"Blast you, Liz," I said, to make her look at me, and see I was smiling too.

So we both burst out laughing.

"Well, Sue mightn't have been taken so seriously, don't you think, Liz? And you'd have been talking to her all the time, and I'm not one for sharing you with her. She has you all the week. Anyway, Limp's up for it all and that's why. I want him to size it up. *Qui morituri* and all that, Liz. Here he is hailing the new Caesars, the very people he might have to become a gladiator for. Or that I might have to become a gladiator for."

"All right," said Liz, quietly. "Let's go for him."

Limp came. He was inclined to hang behind us as we asked questions. Limp, as I've hinted, had become a sort of independent spectator in the world, set apart, sacrificial enough to bother me. I said to myself, I'm taking Limp to tennis this afternoon and to hell with it. Let's enjoy ourselves, at least.

But in the meantime we asked these questions and got our answers. Terrible answers. We went to the Nowhere Plaza. My name for it. And stood about on the concrete. On the wrong side of the gorgeous windows. Everybody was willing to utter loud and clear. We didn't have any difficulty of silence.

". . . What, do them good. Makes men of them, chum. Can't say I've thought about it, much. My children are only in primary yet. Fair? Course it's fair — everybody's the same chance, haven't they?

We had to do it; why not you? Gotta stop 'em, stop 'em there or 'ere, simple as that. Go tomorrow, mate, if I was twenty. Oh, never think o' them things, love, too much trouble — the price o' meat, that's my worry. Got lots to do this morning. Never give to charities meself. What per cent you gettin' on this? When I was your age, lad, I was making for Mary's house in Cairo. Do you good, too. Stay with America, got to; where the strength is — they know what they're about. Don't know any that's been called up. It's like motor accidents, happens to other folk. Consciences? They got no consciences, don't tell me. What ya want a conscience at twenty for? I gotta be in time for the big match; ask me again, will ya? Gotta have a coffee before they shut down. Doesn't affect me; I've only a cuppla girls. Chickening, are you? I know a boy was killed there; reg'lar; just one of those things. Young men, too. Don't know what they're coming to. Gone soft, I think. Gotta be patriotic. Why do you ask? I'm busy."

But there was one woman. "My son," she said, and she walked on a step, stood sideways to us. She worked over her coat for a hankie. Then she gave up and almost covered her face with both her hands, but conquered that. She took the step back to us.

"Michele and I — we have to go and see him every Wednesday — and take things — but what's the use? Brain shot away — he's a vegetable. It's Michele I'm brokenhearted for. Michele's his wife. Why did they bring him back? Or tell us at all? Did they think — "

Michele came up and took her by the arm. "I got the meat. There's only the *TV Times* to get now. What you cryin' for? Come on now, Mum. Not here."

The man who said about Mary's house, I asked him what he did. "Sir," I said.

"Young man," said he, "I'm a judge. I'm waiting for my wife, that's all. Some rather special coffee she wants."

And he put on this theatrical stare of a man exalted on the public gaze all the time. Bent his stare, too, so as to bear down on us, quizzically. He meant us to move away first. Or to freeze the gut out of us, benignly. I didn't know a thing about Mary's house, and I suppose he was counting on our ignorance.

We drew away from the Nowhere Plaza.

I said, "I'm sorry, you guys."

But they were sorry, too. They didn't want to speak, and I hadn't the sense to say nothing, because I'd brought them there.

"How ever could anybody full of ideals fight for that but only against it?" I said, in delirium. "So blank! Let's all go to tennis, shall we, this afternoon?"

But Liz wouldn't have it.

I told them what Dad said about the uselessness of protesting. And because their sympathies were out, and they were my best friends, I told them his story. It was on my mind.

Then we all scattered like the disciples after Gethsemane. The world, surely it couldn't be so full of Judases? Why should we fight for them, by will or nill?

And then Michele and her proxy mum. I wonder if there was any hankie in that pocket after all? She might have come out not looking for any grief, or to get away from it. And we to surprise her into it again.

15

Limp wouldn't go to tennis either. Sprung on me that he and his mum were off on holiday somewhere, that they always went at that time of year — though it was early October, and he'd been at school then, previously. He'd be in touch with me, he said. About as personal as an insurance man was what he sounded. I was soured.

"Course you will," I said. "Why wouldn't you, ever?"

He said nothing.

"You haven't gone and volunteered, have you?"

"No, can't."

"Thought not. That's what Liz said."

"Anyway," he said, "don't worry if you don't hear from me for a week or two."

I hadn't any intention of worrying and I had to go to tennis that Saturday afternoon.

"So long, Limp. Don't mope your holiday away. And don't go to school by mistake."

He must have thought me flippant, as it turned out. There was something on his mind. But how could I know what? I just thought it was all this registering and all the waiting to be drawn like a goose or a lottery ticket. Off I went to tennis.

When I took on the H.S.C. in earnest again, they persuaded me to give up the job I got. But you get pretty, pretty dismal when you're hemmed in by the smiles of a happy family and nothing else but textbooks, textbooks. Paralyzed is what you get, and your head sinks into your naval. So every Saturday I went to tennis. There was a bird there, and Rod and Perce and I were collaborating in the study of this bird.

This bird I'm speaking of didn't mean to live beyond thirty, and her name was Angela. There wouldn't be anything worth living for after that, she said, so you can see what she was after, can't you? Her hair was long as the way to Tipperary, and just as full of wilderness, but she brushed it and brushed it in front of your eyes till it leaped at you, shining like a horse's back. Her face wasn't too remarkable, but then you didn't see all that much of it; and her nose was eaten away to nothing in her eagerness and her hurry through life. She was like the ambulance siren going by — everybody took notice.

"Know Jacqueline Morris?" she suddenly said to Perce, once.

"In the Biblical sense?" Perce asked.

It surprised me, his knowledge of the Bible. But it didn't surprise Angela.

"What's that?" she snapped, till she was sure he'd said it. "I wouldn't know a thing about that," said Angela, with vast satisfaction.

That Saturday she was partnered with me in a club tournament, and as I was four years younger than

Angela she didn't like it much. The motherly ones, they like it quite a lot to have a budding boy for a partner, but if I'd been an old lady with a teacup I couldn't have been more unwelcome to Angela. I tried telling her about Limp and the Nowhere Plaza, because I couldn't shake those things off.

"Funny thing." said Angela. "You'd hardly credit it, but I've never had a soldier for a boy friend. I got a feeling a soldier would kind of suit me, don't you think? Kind of suit me? My very style?"

"No," I said, and she looked affronted. "Khaki's a bit rough on the skin, that's all."

"It isn't a risk," Angela said. "What are you thinking of?"

Well, I could see we weren't thinking about the same thing, and it made me nervous. When my turn came to serve I had to talk to myself, to develop a force of concentration. The sheer responsibility of getting the game started again. If I served a string of double faults, the other three would be standing around, saying nothing, with rackets in their hands, feeling foolish. They might as well have come out to see a reed shaken by the wind as to play tennis. It was like suddenly being left with the world on your shoulders, while Atlas had gone for a pee. So I exhorted myself, with the ball above my head.

This tickled Angela.

"Do you always speak to yourself," she shouted, "when you're playing tennis?"

She wanted me to say yes, so I did, to hit it off with Angela. In the urgency of conversation the exact truth isn't on.

Angela shot me this very relieved merry look, as if, driven into a corner, I'd up and confessed to potency at least. It was a swing of the pendulum, where she'd doubted if there was one.

"I wonder," she began to say, as she tossed me a ball, as we changed courts, as she wiped her hot hand on her pants, "if I'll get what I want? You know, you could be good, real good.

"If you ask me," she said, once, though I wasn't asking her, "in my opinion you're just sure to be a sooner. I bet you're a sooner, Guthrie."

"What's a sooner?" I said.

Well, in the stateliest way Angela just shut up, turned, and walked to the net.

"Come on. Tell me," I said.

But that conversation was at an end. I served a great deal better as the day wore on and it was many many months before my own life taught me what she meant. And she was right. But if Angela can't explain, why then neither can I. I'm far shier than Angela. It'll dawn on you, if you're curious — or married.

Of course I had to take Angela home. She was expecting it, and it's a thing that anybody would do for his partner, and such a partner. She had this droopy mouth and her lips were very, very thin, but she thickened them with a nondescript pale, pale lipstick, which hardly divided the desert from the sown and you didn't know where you were, like a wild goat. She came at you tongue and all, which was new to me. I'll not say I didn't like it. You got pretty sucked in when you were kissing Angela. Though all the time at the back

96

of my head I was feeling shamed and disgraceful. Treacherousness in love, how far on have you got to be before that begins? Oh well, I'd tell Liz about it, most of it, as much as was good for her. We were all on the open market, like day-old chicks. Permissive, that's what everything was.

Angela and I went home by the beaches and there was still some daylight left when we nosed the bomb car Calpurnia out on a grassy cliff, and now that I'd stopped driving and was faced with the whole of Angela's experience I was nearly reduced to shivering. But Angela folded herself alongside me with a comfortable sigh, and what with the weight and the leaning the shivering passed off, but I think she noticed.

"Let's be warm," she said. "Think I could fall asleep. I was up till four."

"What doing?"

"Oh, talking to boys. What did you think we could do till four in the morning?"

So I didn't feel too tied to Angela, even there, even then.

I looked out over the ocean and took in the great sweep of it, the Pacific. She had to look at the dashboard the way her head was fixed. Maybe her eyes were shut, but I don't think so, and I held it against her. Girls, in a way, should abandon themselves. You could hear the surf praying away below us, farther and farther, more and more indistinct, like some vast elongated cathedral aisle with all of the Middle Ages packed inside. And I was lazily stroking Angela's capes and bays and inlets.

All of a sudden she sat up like a seal on a rock and pushed my hand away down and blurted out, "That's my appendix and you must get off it."

She was forbidding me to stroke her flaming appendix?

I knew well enough that Angela's appendix was as sound as a rabbit's and that I wasn't stroking it. All that horsing about the tennis court. I suppose it's the only bit of a woman's anatomy that's passed for general conversation, or even for exigency? Or is it? Liz wasn't aware she had one, I was sure of that; yet Liz wasn't half as elastic as Angela, yet.

"Whenever the boys get as far as my appendix, that's it, it's the end. That's as far as they go."

So there you have it. A sort of a bloody Plimsoll line was old Angela's appendix. Who would have thought to find her so shipshape? I bet you, when you got below it, Angela sank at once. She was a troopship, like the *Birkenhead*. Plenty of other chaps were giving her what she wanted, but I don't fancy any company there, not much. And that's not at all unusual, or prim, but only sense. Team spirit, sometimes, can be out of place, even in a boisterous and sporty age. I just hung on for a bit under her left teat till I thought all this out, and then we went home.

She was pretty quiet. She didn't tell me any more of her geography.

16

ANGELA'S APPENDIX burst on me that Saturday in October, and I gave Rod a short account of it, a very short account, because of professional ethics.

"She's pretty hot stuff," I said, "this tennis partner."

"Hot stuff! That's how I like 'em, boy."

I saw I'd have to go deeper into it. Rod hadn't really cottoned on. He was just being polite. He poked at our fence and gave this very loud burp.

"I think," I said, "she's a nymphomaniac."

"What's that?" said Rod.

Well, I'd looked it up, so I told him and he made off.

He must have thought about it, though. One night he borrowed Calpurnia to take a date out. Then Perce rang up and asked me to go to a drive-in. *G.I. Blues* it was.

"Rod has Calpurnia," I said.

"Well, so what? There's my bus."

So we went, and after the show I was walking back from the loo when a bloke said to me, "You on the staff here?" and for the hell of it I said I was. "There's a breakdown over there," he said.

Perce and I went over, and there of course were Carlson and Calpurnia and Angela in a neat little huddle together.

"Lousy bastard," I said to Rod, glaring at Calpurnia.

And I said to Angela, "How's your ruddy appendix, girl? Nicely tickled up?"

I didn't mean to mince my words, but there you are, I minced them. And this bint Angela, she just laughed and laughed. Struck her as hellish funny.

Then Limp came back and I had to go to town with him and we were sitting in the train when he told me.

"I haven't registered," said Limp.

"Not registered at all?"

"No, not at all. How could you do it by half?"

"But, good God, Limp, I've got to get used to this. Haven't seen you for weeks and you been doing this. Why, oh why didn't you tell me? They'll put you in jail and treat you awful grim. Here I've been on the razzle, too. Been living it up."

I meant how I could maybe have helped.

"Had to think it out for myself," he said. "I did keep Mum posted. Till she was desperate." He looked at me, empty-faced. Limp hadn't been enjoying himself on holiday. The train went lurching about and interrupting, not giving a damn for our concerns.

"I don't want to serve bad policies, and blokes that don't know what they're at, and don't care. To put my life and conscience in *their* hands, enslave myself. When ninety-nine per cent of Australians are living at peace, and thinking peace. Ninety-nine point nine per cent. It can't be right. Nobody is really implicated in this but us."

"So first of all, you were thinking to register as a conscientious objector, I suppose?"

"Yes," he said, "I was."

"Then why didn't you?"

"I've just stated my objection. They wouldn't call it conscience."

We were on our way to town to see his solicitor. Here was my mate Limp with a solicitor of his own already, while I was giving all my attention to kids' things like exams and tennis and women. He'd gone and got out of my grip, at a stroke. I suddenly felt the need of a cigarette, to draw some meditative puffs and not say anything and let the damn pavements slide, slide, and the platforms, and all the smug red roofs.

"I don't see why they should trap me, even into explaining myself."

"Trap you?"

"Yes. Nobody else does."

"Does what?"

"Explains himself. *Qui s'excuse s'accuse.* You can catch any man on anything if you ask him why he does it. Why are you going to town, now?"

"To see your solicitor."

"You don't care if you never see my solicitor. Isn't it because you want to protect me? Because you feel sorry for a stranger in the land? Feel guilty about getting me expelled? Feel we've both got to deal with this call-up? Together?"

"Oh, hell," I said. "You been happy here, Limp?"

"Yes, mostly happy."

I knew he couldn't be too happy when his father drowned, and with his mum left in a cheerless life, and with other people's wars to fight. But at least when you plastered statues there were kicks in it and all the callous boss guys had to notice you for once and you didn't feel too down. But it was all mixed up. I didn't want to be the sap drawn out of the ballot either, for sure. I just sat staring in perplexity, enjoying it all as little as my cigarette. Maybe I should join the C.M.F. — which was the territorial side of the army, and you couldn't be sent abroad but were buggered about at home for three times as long, instead. To hell with that for a lark. A shallow way to bribe young men, playing on their wishes and their liberty. And though I wouldn't have done it, I wasn't damning Limp for not registering. He was making a mistake, but men made mistakes in war, too, causing pitiless havoc. Nobody has to think now that Gallipoli was a good thing. Nobody but Mutch and his mentality, and it's stupid to expect me and my mates to share it.

"Still," I said, and he understood me, "this country hasn't done you too badly. It's home to you. Maybe the question really is whether you and I owe it something back. I'm just considering," I said.

"Let's both go and join up then. Instead of going to the solicitor's."

I looked out and saw the wind blowing at a girl's skirt, the very first thing the wind ever does in the modern world and I'm obliged to it. I looked again and saw how well her face agreed with the wind's keen interest. She was very pretty, and serious, as well.

Like the Blessed Damosel come true. Clean eyes with a lot of love in them. She stood for the joy of the living world to me, even if she very smartly vanished and I'll never see her again.

"No," I said, "we'll not. We'll not join up. It just isn't on. We can't hold our lives dangling indefinitely just because of this. I couldn't join up. I'll have to be balloted first, and I know I won't like it. But I suppose I'll go."

"It's just the press gang over again. Seizing anybody you can get with the form of law."

"You'd think any decent democracy would fling it out at the next election."

"Bad government and apathy, they go together. Nobody cares. It isn't important to them."

You know how you can think of anything in a train and go around and around? For some reason I was thinking of Mister Mary Ann, our headmaster. That headmaster used to talk about integrity. And then went bobbing and time-serving to his council, putting his integrity at their disposal. Prime ministers, they're apt to do the same. They try to be all things to all men, till their faces can really stink with honesty and earnestness. And we've got to shine, have we, we young fellows, with all their hypocritical patriotism, like a mirror held in the hand?

"And so," Limp was saying, "first of all I meant to volunteer and sweeten the thing for myself. But they couldn't have me that way. There was no provision in the Act. So I thought of objection, but with objection — "

"You could have managed to convince them very

well. Your religion's almost unique here, and you could string out verses of the Bible like sausages."

"That's just it," Limp said. "It all stinks. For my religion's the same as theirs. We're all — "

"What do you mean?"

"We're all agnostic. Even if there's a God, we've nothing to do with Him. We're all in a claptrap conveyor-belt consumer's world, and that's all. This people honoreth, honoreth, what is it?"

"This people honoreth me with their lips but their heart is far from me."

"Right," said Limp. "And nowhere farther than in a law court. Very sad places. All the trappings left, but hollow. Like a temple in African sand to Venus Cytherea. God's name shouted every day, but who believes it? I couldn't go on with that. I couldn't suffer the shame of a religious objection."

"So?"

"That way, my conscience — can't you see? — would be up before Annas and Caiaphas. They'd see the reflection of their own expediency. For who are they? Public men in matters of conscience are pretty sure to be hypocrites, and mouth the expected thing. Careerists, not Sir Thomas Mores. Nobody questions what's expected, see. Why should I go through with that pantomime, and play the villain in it?"

"Well, you could be Sir Thomas More yourself."

"No," said Limp, turning and staring out of the window. "Haven't the courage. Haven't the courage," he muttered. "I'm no better than my judges."

"So you haven't registered at all?"

"And so I haven't registered, and it means we're on

the move. That's really what I wanted to tell you. Maybe you'll kindly witness a deed of sale at our solicitor's, and not mind doing what his typists could do. We're selling our house, and leaving. Mum will be there; she's going straight there."

The electricity poles and the houses racketed by.

"Limp," I said, "old man, are you happy about this?"

"Not happy," he said. "Happier than I was, that's all. Choosing between evils."

"You could have taken your matric, got a scholarship, gone on with your degree. They would have deferred you."

"I would have been binding myself, binding myself under deep obligations to the very things I'm objecting to. The time would have come when I had to face it that those who paid for my degree were asking unconscionable things of me. My answer would have been less clear and clean then than it is now. And in the meantime I'd be held on end for years, waiting to see what they'd do with me."

"Limp, as I've said, often, I've no doubt of your conscience. My own conscience answers it, every step. But there's one thing. Your conscience can't sleep. And how are you going to answer it as it turns and tells you — as it tells you you haven't registered, that you've disobeyed, and that you're living on the run? Much like, oh, much like Ned Kelly."

Limp shuffled there, a bit uncomfortably, and it frightened me. I didn't say it to make him uncomfortable. "Oh," he said, "you're right, of course. I'll try and do good things. To atone to myself. Won't make a fortune or anything. I have a plan. Hermits fled from the world. I *can't* find a perfect answer! Guth," he cried, "you don't expect me to find a perfect answer?"

The perfect answer was with the politicians, to abolish a bad law.

17

"Liz, are you busy?"

It was study-break vac, the week before the H.S.C., and I suppose she was working.

"Liz, it's a world now where you don't know what your own friends are doing, or thinking, or even your own family. Oh, Liz, I had to phone you, even if you are working very hard. Limp hasn't registered. He hasn't registered at all. He'll land in jail."

There was a great silence at the other end.

"May I come and see you, Liz? Now?"

"Yes. G'bye. Hello? Are you there? You aren't telling everybody this, are you? And over the phone?"

"Oh, no, Liz. Only you. See you. Thanks. G'bye."

Liz said, "What we're going to do is get back in Calpurnia and go and see your dad."

I didn't argue. We did just that. I'd come back from town by myself, thinking all about it. Limp in the street had embraced me in the continental fashion, or tried to, and his mum had patted my hand.

"Will be all reight, all reight," she said.

She would have said more, but he cut her off.

"I'll write you, maybe, after a while. Come on, Mum."

"You're off now?" I said.

But I was only talking to an approaching passer-by, who couldn't answer me. Mutely agreed, if you like, and pressed on his way. Perhaps I should have phoned Dad there and then, but right action, it's a difficult thing. And I tend to cover up by joking, Liz says, as though I didn't care about anything, which is not so. One of the first things I noticed about Liz was that she was better at knowing what to do. This day she made me drive past Limp's place on the way to see Dad. It was all locked up, with a FOR SALE notice still on the fence.

"But it's sold," I said. "The buyers were there. And a very funny thing, Liz. I was going to witness the deed of sale and he stopped me, the lawyer stopped me."

"Oh, of course," Liz said. "A minor?"

"A bloody minor," I said. "The law can dress me up in khaki to shoot, burn, and slay in the name of Australia, but I am too young to know when a chap's writing his name. I could cack myself," I said to Liz. Seized the chance of a four-letter word on her. Kill, burn, and slay are no four-letter words, oh, no. But "cack yourself" is.

"We'll have to get in touch with that lawyer, I suppose," said Liz, very mildly, skillfully overlooking the implicit foulness of everything.

And it was what Dad said, too, but I couldn't recall his name, that lawyer's. "He's a tall man. Pleasant to speak to. And those house deeds have always been with him. Limp's folk just stayed on with him. But I can't think what he's called."

All this magnificent information they simply rejected. Liz looked at Dad as if he'd been talking.

"What street was it, boy?"

"Oh, Bridge Street. Scottish House."

"Now let's look up the solicitors on the pink pages."

After one or two phone calls they got the lawyer and he wasn't very keen to give his client's address, but when we said again that my name had blamelessly escaped his documents, he said Poste Restante, Launceston.

And that's as far as we could get. The three of us were walking about with the whole house to do it in. Nobody else, it being early afternoon, was at home.

"You think he's crazy, Dad?"

"Oh, I wouldn't have done it," Dad said.

"But you — "

"Yes, I know. Nothing I did was against the law, nor was it in question. Here it is. Of course," he said, "in our war you could hardly have done this. Because of rationing, for one thing. And because we felt that Hitler was compelling us, not our own government. Yet why be surprised? Destruction keeps on improving, and so must the protests against it. And this is deliberate protest, not just scrimshanking."

"I suppose," said Liz, "that quite a few boys might just fail to register."

"Yes, and I suspect they're not out to cop them very much. They've more than enough and just toss for them. Limp isn't likely to walk into a police station, is he? If he'd intended that, he would have done it here."

"You don't think we should go, do you?"

"Young lady," Dad said, "I think we're compounding a felony."

"But, Dad, you don't want us all to go — "

"No, quite true, I don't. I'm sure we can sleep quiet if not guiltless. We'll never land in jail for this. But he might. And what to do? You see," Dad said, "by moving he's put himself off a bit from discovery, certainly. Nobody knows him in Tasmania. But if he *is* found, it'll be the worse for him for flitting. At any rate, let's not mention it to anybody."

"No, Dad, but — it's not just another thing to forget about and leave to somebody else, is it? Is there nothing we can do?"

"The only thing we could do would be to get to Limp and talk to him."

"I'll do that then," I said. "Oh, I'll sit the exams first."

"The police," said Liz, "could find out as easily as we did."

"And far more easily where he is exactly. We'll just have to hope that nothing prompts them to ask. Till we can get at him. By letter, maybe," he said, appealing to me. "See if we can persuade him to register, at least. He's making it hard for himself. There are ways of doing this."

"Of not registering?"

"No, of objecting. In the meantime, he's not only cut himself off from discovery, but also from help if he's caught. He's merely a malefactor, down there. Up

110

here, he's our friend. There were lawyers," Dad said, "who were very good friends to me when I needed it. Very good friends, indeed. Clear men, as clear on principle as law. But they never can do much if you act for yourself and ask them after."

On the very first day of the H.S.C. I turned out of our gate just after lunch in Calpurnia, meaning to get to the exam hall nice and early and take everything quietly. Glancing down the street for any traffic, I did notice a mini parked farther down, but thought nothing of it. When I looked in the mirror, as you do when you start off, I saw that the mini was close and drawing past. It was the coppers, and they signaled me in. Hell, I thought, it would be today. But I was still pretty confident, for I'd only started off, and maybe they just checked on all the old bombs by routine. They'd find Calpurnia in good nick: brakes, tires, and all. Even the horn was good for a solid peep.

You don't say anything when a copper draws up on you, nothing at all. He was watching me carefully, with a gleam in his eye, as though we were playing poker and him with the best cards.

"Got your license handy?"

He was a sergeant. His mate was in the mini, watching.

I had my hand on the hilt of my license already, so I drew it smartly as all three musketeers. I'm not versed in the ways of coppers but, still, there was something unexpected. Why did he say "handy"? And why hadn't he called me "driver," for instance, or "lad," a thing they're very apt to do if they feel they have you and there's nothing you can really do but pray. So I just handed him my license, and waited, looking at him all the time with earnest deference, taking him seriously. He kept turning my license over and back, and he said, kind of thoughtfully, "You got a pal called Limp, by any chance?"

Looked straight at me then. Soon saw that I'd already answered.

"Yes, I have," I said very candidly.

"Know where he's gone?"

"No," I said, "I don't know where he's gone. He said good-bye to me last Wednesday in town."

"Yes, I know," he said, but I doubt if he genuinely did. He gave me back my driving license. "And you've no idea where he's gone, or what he means to do?"

"No," I said, "honestly I haven't. I wish I did have."

"You and he were lately expelled from school together, weren't you? Insulting the governor? Something like that?"

"Yes, Sergeant, sure we were expelled. But it wasn't for insulting the governor, and it wasn't Limp's fault, it was mine. Has nothing to do with his going away."

"How can you be sure now, I wonder?"

"Because, because . . . His going away was a clean surprise to me, Sergeant. Didn't know till last Wednesday, either."

"Sudden, was it? However, he had his mother with him, I think. And that's good company for most young men."

"Oh, yes. You don't think they've run away with money or anything, do you?"

"No," he said, not to be caught, looking out of the side of his eye. "And neither do you, do you?"

I didn't answer that, directly.

"I know he's not a criminal. His father was drowned," I said, "last year. They came from Hungary, refugees. He's a good chap, Limp," I said, "oh, don't — "

And then I looked at him, very concerned. I couldn't say, "Don't be hard on him."

"And you don't know where he is?"

"No," I said, "I swear I don't."

"All right, lad, off you go."

I must have done one hell of an exam. If Limp wrote to me now, should I tell them? Should I tell Dad and Liz? As soon as the exams were over, I'd be after him. If I had the money, that is. Should I write to Poste Restante, Launceston, or not? What the heck should I do? And how had they got to know so early? I hoped I hadn't given anything away. I went over it again and again to check, while all the others in the exam hall were writing like fury, making themselves terribly unreal to me. I sometimes imagined they dazzled my ears into singing. Here I was mixed up with the police. I sat that exam, as you might say, in the police of the weather. There were all sorts in that hall — men, women, Chinamen, and swarthy macaronis, brightening their hopes with laborious answers. And they didn't know that a villain was sitting among them.

18

IMMEDIATELY AFTER my exams finished, it rained pretty
hard in the night. I knew because I could see it, but
better still because the creek at the foot of our garden
was running with a very pleasant sound, and the trees
had a fresh, wet music — as though you'd just been
syringing your ears. But I knew for sure about the rain
when Cam Sutton, next door, came sauntering down
in his dressing gown for the milk and paper, with
his pajamas stuffed into his big seaboots. This country
in its ease of life can surprise you into admiration, and
I gave him a slow handclap with every step he took,
making sure he didn't hear.

I was sitting on our verandah studying the employment columns and waiting for the rest of the paper
to dry, even if it took all day. Idleness had stolen upon
me. It was good to be shut of all the excessive toil of
the H.S.C. But if I wanted to go to Tasmania, and be
in time, I'd have to make a bit of money fast. There
was full employment, of course, and I could get in on
it whenever I liked.

After a long time there were only two jobs that stood
out, one that I fancied and one that I didn't. The local

golf course was looking for a laborer. That was the one
I fancied. I knew the pro, and most of the boys, and I
agree with those who think that golf courses with
trees are the only places left where you can have
the decorous vistas of eighteenth-century England and
hear the birds like blackbird and thrush. I bet it never
occurred to Capability Brown when he laid his poetry
into the landscape that a time would come when nobody gave a damn for hearing the thrush. We haven't
got song thrushes, but magpies with the wind behind
them can spray the world with their voices.

But, thinks I, that's just it. It's cowardly. You're
escaping. You've always been a bit quick to follow
your whims and get out from under. Well, I could have
argued with myself then, for I've been giving you the
answer, but instead I turned to the other job. It said:

Opportunity keen young man; sell leading encyclopedia suburbs; on commission basis; own
hours; earn up to $36 weekly.

No, I'm *not* saying I liked it. But I'd be my own
boss. Practically. And with Calpurnia, I could stuff a
suburb full of encyclopedias in two weeks at most. It
only needed twenty-six suburbs in the whole of Sydney
and there was a year's steady salary in it. If I wanted,
and I didn't. Enterprise was what was needed and I
had that, surely. It had been a curse to me so far, but
things could boomerang — like swearing, which isn't
much use to you when you're a littlie, but when you're
grown-up it seems to be no handicap. Selling encyclopedias was a lurk that students got up to every year

at this time, and I'd heard John talking about it. Altogether I thought I could make it and go to Tasmania when I had money enough. So I shouldered Calpurnia and off I set for famous Sydney Town.

Of course I could see the fellow was a phony straight-away. Trouble is, to a teen-ager, everybody is. It's like looking at Chinamen. To me there's just something plausible about the big-business look, well-ironed, with a detergent whiteness about the eye, as if you were always coming so clean, so clean. They're usually bronzed and wizened guys, too, committed to lasting at all cost, like an apple that's been in the sea for a month. Hair receding, but very spruce, and genial matching live-and-let-live crow's-feet propping the eyes. That's how this rocker looked anyway, Lew Penny-feather, of the crisp handshake. He'd even kept his first name young, can't you see? But he was old, he was old, with a great big desk, two or three telephones, and a pad. Nothing else. A real executive's desk it was. He passed everything on. That didn't prevent his desk from being the biggest in the outfit.

His secretary called him Mr. Pennyfeather in a quizzy sort of a way, as if she respected him for his wit. But then she had to speak through an awful lot of mascara and eyebrow pencil, all brewed up together. She made up for this Egyptology by going short on her dress, which was really skimpy, and grew most interesting when she crossed her legs, and it made her legs look longer, and her knees clumsier, more Doric, than the rest of her. The rest of her was Caesar's wife, but those knees reassured you. They were well matched. Not the knees, but Lew and Jane. He called her Miss Tooke, though she wore a host of wedding rings and must have married a better name than that.

"Well, young man, what can I do for you, sir?"

Brisk and amused he was, living his reputation. Benign smile exuded for about two beats of the bar. Then there was a minim rest, or something. Three/four time.

"About selling encyclopedias," I said. "Your advertisement."

The tempo changed, and the music was louder. "Oh, got to be on your toes for that post. Got to know the selling line. And be familiar with the article. And there's the added consideration of the requirements of your buyer. Got to think of all that. Oh, dear me. Don't you worry. Housewives on their own doorsteps, and careful of the purse strings, they're hard as nails. Hard as nails, I tell you. Mr. — er — er — don't imagine they'll fall for every handsome young man that shows up. No, sir. This is a post for a seasoned salesman, Mr. Guthrie, a responsible post, serving the education of a nation . . ."

He'd been studying the ice-cream ads, obviously, or listening to parliamentary broadcasts.

". . . demanding resource, zeal, courage, dedication, loyalty to the job. You're too young to have developed those qualities as I would like them."

I was too young to assume them right enough. And even the army didn't ask for anything more. Except your life, except your life, except your life.

"I'm sorry," he was saying. "But what experience do you have, as a matter of interest? What's your record? Great Public School?"

I was too disgusted by now.

117

"Yes," I said. "I was expelled."

He took it on the crow's-feet, I must say; real live-and-let-live he was about it. "Go on," he said, scraping the stoicism out of his vocal cords. "No matter for that." Hoarse, like a roustabout with an awfully good heart, in the movies.

He lowered his eyes, though, and tidied his blotter, and when he looked up the crow's-feet had contracted. Must have been taking me more seriously. Could even have been thinking if I was as big a rogue as himself.

"Mr. Pennyfeather," I said, and I laid it on for him, "I've imagination and enterprise, all pent up inside me. School doesn't give the scope for it, Mr. Pennyfeather. You can't apply it to quadratics and things like regular verbs. You can to irregular ones, of course." I was driven to caricature; for there's a witless cunning about many a successful man, and it doesn't call out your best responses much. "I reckon if I took some of your encyclopedias around the suburbs in Calpurnia — Calpurnia's my car and quite a lady — I reckon I'd apply the old shrewdness to gauge up the people I met. I could sell them a thing or two."

I was horrified to hear myself. As if I'd got around on his side of the desk already. Moved the mock-heroic in me, he sure did.

Of course, the upshot was I got the job, or post, as he called it. When he began capering about with his switches, and said, "Oh, Miss Tooke, get me P. G. Waterhouse, the big contractors, will you?" I knew it was in the bag. He called it checking up on my credentials with my former employer. Even had the hide to say he knew Mr. Waterhouse. But on the phone, of course, he kept out the back-slapping. One big contractor to another. And when he drifted back to me across his desk, he said, "Well, congratulations, old boy, Mr. Waterhouse spoke very highly of you. Up and coming, he said. Too good to sell encyclopedias, but that was just his little joke."

Then came all the serious business instructions, cut very near the bone; though it was always the housewives that were hard, you had to remember that.

The way this guy worked it, he couldn't lose. It was only commission. Two-volume encyclopedias they were, cheap, on poor paper, potted. You strained your eyes for the information you got. It was only for school, and not even that. But in sales know-how he put it on a par with the Britannica. And when I slipped in about Calpurnia, that did it for me.

All that guy wanted was a fleet of other folks' cars. I didn't let him see Calpurnia. He didn't want to, I'm sure. Guys in the city don't give a damn where your car is, even if it's earning a ten-quid fine or being towed away while you help them on with their careers. So I told him it was a small Triumph. And it was, wasn't it?

"Triumph Herald?" he said.

But I reckoned I wasn't called on to testify. He kept as vague as decency about his side of the transaction. "Transaction" was one of his well-bred words: like "obtain," "require," "stuff yourself."

I was glad to bundle Calpurnia off home with a wisp or two of his encylopedias. The city was no place for her. But the farther I trundled on my way, the less pleased I felt.

I drew in at the curb to think about it.

119

You're not really thinking this is a job you've taken?
I said. *Yes, I do. In a city there's all sorts of jobs and
this is one of them. But you don't really think these
folks really need your encyclopedias, do you?* Well,
I said, *take brushes. There's folks selling brushes from
door to door, and ice cream from door to door, and nobody really needs them but they buy them. Even a
lousy encyclopedia's a better buy than a brush. You
can't read a brush.*

I was determined to be serious about it. *Well,* I said,
*you could try it out. Here's a house. You could sell
them two of your encyclopedias. If you're in earnest
about it, that is. So I could,* I said.

I looked over at the back seat and I looked to see if
there was anything coming up the road; or if anything
was happening to the roof of the house; but all was still
as buried Troy. There was just no sign in the street at
all. So there was no getting away from it. The time
had come to sell an encylopedia or to stop forever selling encyclopedias. Quite a solemn moment.

So I got out of Calpurnia and walked up the drive.
Very quietly. I rang the bell. Touched my tie. I did
notice that my mouth was dry as a real good sherry.
Tio Pepe, maybe. After all, you can't break off the habit
of a lifetime just like that.

The lady that came to the door could see it was a
salesman, I think. Or would she? The door was one of
those indeterminate front doors on the side of the house,
but I'd left all the encyclopedias in Calpurnia. She
smiled. She must have been about thirty-six and that
morning it looked a mighty pleasant age to be. I liked
her. She was working about the house, I know, but she

hadn't any curlers in her hair. I thought, you belong with the wise virgins: your lamps are always trimmed.

"Good morning, madam," I said.

"Good morning. Can I do anything for you?"

If I wasn't quick, it would go the opposite way.

"Oh, I was just going along the street trying to interest people in something. First of all, have you any children? Please?"

She looked concerned. The smile had gone and left her face still gentle.

"Yes," she said, "there's one playing in the back garden, and there's two at school. But — "

"Well," I said, "don't ever buy them any encyclopedias that they'll sell you from door to door. It's a racket, lady, in my opinion, or this one is. It's a racket. Don't have anything to do with it. The folks that own them don't really care, and that's the truth. They're taking a cut at your money. But bookshops now, they're the places. Nobody ever owned a bookshop without caring about books. Go there, lady. I'm in a hurry now, or I'd tell you more. Sorry to trouble you. Goodbye. And good luck."

"Are you all — wait till I get you a glass of water. Won't take a — "

But I waved her words away and went ahead with my adjurations. It had to be said. I finished it halfway down the path. After I shut the gate, I sprinted for Calpurnia and made straight for the golf course.

She was still at the door as I passed. Open-mouthed more than was becoming. But she waved to me. There's tenderness about, if you need it at times. A glimpse of soft hearts. And I like them.

19

I GOT THE JOB, and took one step back into a greener
century, but not for long.

One of the members of this golf club was a lieutenant colonel, retired, and quite often throughout the
year he would earn his pension by being called Colonel
around the place. It was stupid of me, when I was rak-
ing a bunker and changing the sprinklers, to ask him
one day what he thought of all this conscription now.
I'll just tell you what he said, while I stood there, miserably, wishing my rake was a piece of artillery, for the
argument's sake. I'm a peaceful cove, didn't want to
shoot him down.

"How old are you, boy?" said he.

"Eighteen," I said.

So, because I was eighteen, he started praising himself.

"It takes a man," he said, "to be a soldier. Australia,
thank God, is a man's land. Men shouldn't need to be
conscripted. It's a great privilege to fight for one's
country. Anybody who isn't prepared to fight and die
for his country should be simply ignored. Every ex-

serviceman is proud of his heritage and not only that but also of the part he played in making this country safe for democracy. And prosperous. Prosperous enough for even you to live in, boy. To rake bunkers in, and that sort of thing."

He was passing this advice from his left hand to his right hand per medium of the head of his nine iron, which he was patting his right hand with. I was just standing there. I wasn't patting anything. Thought if I moved at all he might give me C.B.

So I said, "Yes, sir." And looked for a bunker one hole farther back. He's plentiful, too, up and down this great heritage of ours, or country, as I prefer to call it, and which I think I already prize and appreciate a sight better than he does. But actually, outside music hall, to hear those mouthings — though I knew they went on — produces the effect of cannon fire: stuns you. It isn't serious in itself. For a man like that is incapable of seriousness. But he's got to be taken very seriously, because he's a lieutenant colonel, retired, and his lack of penetration is widespread and influential. For the rest of that day I was thoughtful at my bunkers, and sad, and didn't speak to any other golfers. Limp, or anybody else, in tackling that lot alone, had undertaken a losing battle. I could see that. Lieutenant colonels, I could see very well, were kept inert in blinkers, like horses. The thing was occupational.

One day when I got home there was a letter from Limp, which I must confess surprised me — so soon, at any rate. I thought he would just stoically vanish. *Dear Guth, I want to see you, and soon. I am at the Milk Board's place at Back Street, Port Macquarie, every weekday between eleven and twelve. I don't work for the Milk Board, of course. Please come. Next week if you can. Yours, Limp.*

So he'd gone north after all, and the address in Launceston was simply a blind — unless his mum had gone there, for some reason. And that's how it turned out, for she had a cousin there. The Revolution had scattered them, like the Jews.

So I counted up my money and was paid off, and off I went for Port Macquarie. On the way I thought to myself about Australia, and the call-up, and the plight of young men.

It didn't seem to be an easy world. It was mid-December and the weather uninterruptedly fine. Here was all this country to wage war on. Let them conscript me for that and I might live in it forever. Australia has a sadder greenness than other places, though I hadn't seen any other places then, except in pictures. I've no lack of loyalty to what is my own and beautiful to me. There's a great reverence toward life and when you're young you feel it hard, and one of its main outlets is, and ought always to be, a sheer delight in the visible scene you share. Don't, for God's sake, sneer and say "old hat." You're only cramping yourself. If it ever comes to a question of choosing between the tin-can world and the natural one, then I'll tell you which it is that man will choose: he'll choose the natural one. He'll smash all his tin cans of every description, whether to live in, to ride in, or to eat food out of. If sense and instinct can't make him do it, I'll also tell you what else will: the logic and calamity of his own greed. It's only greed that keeps him back from enjoying the world, and it's only greed that drives him on to the smashing. It's always a question of choosing between the tin-can world and the natural one. And those that choose the natural one are never greedy. Content they are, though.

And as I turned the corners, I belted this out.

And I could be that, I could be well content, but there's only one thing. I've one ambition that eats me up. Ambition's a form of greed. The Grecian urn is mine, my greediness. I'd like to make something of perfect art, so that it could live beyond me. I've no notion at all of the names on war memorials or honor rolls, or of the spurious contemporary brouhaha that nearly all men get embittered in. But to be able to draw a simple line like the line of the Dividing Range or some seacoast — a line that's smooth with immortality. I know perfectly what John Keats was after when he spent his life on this, for it's what he did. He paid his life across a counter, as it were, a most intelligent thing, for it was, with his poetry, his capital. Keats apprehended that nothing less than all of him was needful to the execution of his poetry. And so he was steadily shedding the prurience of Romanticism, till he called his Grecian urn "a friend to man," and that's the warm fruition of any substantial beauty. Yeats found it, late, and he found it perennial. The reaching of it is apt to kill a man, because there's nothing beyond it, for striving at. Well, I would like to reach it, nevertheless.

Of all places at that time, we Guthries liked Port Macquarie best, and I planned to arrive there in the fresh of the early summer morning. I had a foreboding of evil to come, but at least I would enjoy my coming upon that holiday neighborhood, like coming back to Liz again after racketing too long with Angela. So I slept in Calpurnia at Laurieton and that way you don't sleep late in the mornings. I was trundling the coast road while the sun was still bright off the sea. And I stopped, and mused, and got out once or twice.

Before you come to Bonnie Hills there's a treacherous little bay, barred in by magnificent headlands, particularly to the north, and the surf piles in and pummels the beach. The waves one and all are like hills that shape themselves and go, treading each other down. And close in, because of the headlands poking out, you can see leaning pillars of gannets diving and once you've seen the steep flash of that, you won't feel that you've ever seen a white bird before, so to outshine the sea. Gulls are guttersnipes beside them. They ply the length of the Tasman to their rocks in Bass Strait. They're restless, reckless, and victorious birds, and those are the qualities of the sea itself . . . Though sometimes they go blind with hitting it so hard. And then they starve to death.

But what I specially like about that northern headland is that a pair of sea eagles nest there, ospreys, and you can't look seaward for long without seeing them. Not that they're out at sea, but the road is back a bit. And any minute you can catch them, with their bald heads, balancing and blown about in the continual buffeting and unsteadiness of the wind on the precipice. The rocks crumble and the landslides dicker into the sea, but they, like the phrases of Mozart and Haydn, keep continually slipping in. They score the view. You could make a special journey from Sydney and be sure of seeing them. They'd be shuttling back and forth. Like Charon the ferryman, they're forever. They tie me fast to that eastern coast, crawling with spray, flattened into memory beneath them.

When I got to Back Street between eleven and twelve, Limp was there, sure enough, helping with the unloading, a busy man. He made very little sign of seeing me, but I saw that he had, and I didn't want to go and speak to him in there. It was wearisome waiting till finally he came, walking. "Let's have some lunch, shall we?" We tramped around to the main street, making for the nearest hamburger shop.

"Gee, I'm glad to see you," he said, and sighed, and looked pretty grim. "You came in Calpurnia? Nice trip? How long d'you take?"

We were conscious, both of us, of walking about in the midday sun, as though we were mad dogs and Englishmen. Gave us a slinking feeling.

"Limp," I said, "the police were asking me about you, where you'd gone."

"Let's talk about it," said Limp, frightened, but relieved to show it, "after lunch, after we've left Port Macquarie."

"Okay. Let's take one or two hamburgers, and go. A carton of milk coffee and scram, shall we?"

So we did that, hastily. Quite suddenly Port Macquarie had become a place to wipe the dust of your feet from. Nobody even suggested we could go and look at the beach and talk. We had to be on the hop.

"Say," I said, as we walked back, "how'd you get this job?"

Limp shrugged. "Better than the last one I had.

I've only had it a few days. I was drink waiter in a pub, before. They take on extra staff for Christmas. And I happened to hear this man say he wanted a driver for his truck. Dorrigo to here, daily. He was glad to have me. Bed down in Dorrigo. Far better. I like it. The job part of it. We sold our car when Dad went. Didn't know I missed it, till now. Could be a truck driver in the army, fine."

It was the first thing Limp had said about the army. He smiled then. Too wryly, though.

"Could I come up Dorrigo with you?"

"Yes," he said, "that'd be great."

"But what about Calpurnia? Tell you what," I said, "we could put her in a garage overnight to get her exhaust welded. If it doesn't cost too much," I said.

"I could pay," said Limp. "You've come all this way for me."

"It's a small job," I said. "I'll take my gear out. There's not much. But I have a sleeping bag. And toothbrush. Suppose I can sleep at your place?"

"Sure," he said.

So we went up Dorrigo Mountain.

Dorrigo Mountain — if you haven't been there, be ashamed of yourself, sell all that you have and make amends this very summer. A petrol pilgrimage will take you, or a Cook's tour. The road will take you worshiping through a vast green cathedral of rain forest, whose builder and maker is God. And which the Lord of the Hill has placed there for the refreshment of travelers. You know how medieval piety put up bridge-chapels and chapels-of-ease? A sort of motel they were, where needy travelers could turn aside and rest from the heat of the way, and the wilderness of this world. Well, they were small Gothic and that's maybe a bad thing. Their beauty is minuscule, and sometimes the way up the escarpment of the ranges can hem you in like them. Here at Dorrigo God has managed a sense of space. Often enough, the windows of the tall trunks, leaded with branches, where the light is stained with leaves, open onto other green transepts and chapels. You suddenly realize that you're looking across some great Glastonbury Abbey that the centuries have unroofed, whose floor is sunk below your understanding. And perhaps the Bellingen River, so comfortable in its lower valley, gropes unborn in the belly of the mountain. See Dorrigo and die.

Sublimity it is, and caught in a net, and in Australia. Nothing Coca-Cola about it. Go this summer. Just trust in God and see your brakes are fixed. Oh, God, there once again you can pick out what a born Cromwellian soldier I am!

20

AN INTERESTING THING I noticed on the trip to Dorrigo.
I don't know whether it was because I'd sat the H.S.C.
and Limp hadn't. I doubt if that's the reason. What
had happened was that I'd got in front of Limp and he
was looking to me for guidance. There was no good
pretending that it wasn't so. It's got to be borne, that's
all, as a part of growing up. Your other pals like Perce
and Rod fade into the distance, and even parents re-
cede. It's a tossup whether you mean to take Angela
or Liz through life along with you, or some Angela or
Liz. Well, not a tossup as regards Angela, maybe:
she's only an easy lay. There's plenty of that and you
don't have to toss it. Just guard yourself against it,
that's all. In my present circumstances, here where I'm
writing, I can see that a man has need of protection
against such predators. On the road to Dorrigo,
though, she was of small concern, because you don't
find the nymphs among the shepherds anymore, and
for another reason, too.

"You were right," said Limp, "about my conscience.
Mine's been giving me hell. It's too much for me, Guth."

I knew what he meant, and I was anxious for him.

"I thought that if my own mind was clear, it wouldn't matter what anybody else thought. And it doesn't matter what anybody else thinks — and yet it does," he said flatly, staring straight ahead. "What do you think?"

"I would have registered," I said.

"I know you would." He lifted both hands off the wheel. "What do I do, what do I do?" he cried.

"Limp, I'm sure there's nothing to hinder you filling up a form at Bellingen Post Office this very afternoon. You won't be expelled again, or put in jail. Conscription in peacetime, this is a thing that hasn't been tried before and the less persecution and controversy there is about it the better. The better pleased the Canberra boys will be."

"Okay," Limp said, brightening but not very hearty, "we stop at Bellingen."

He was just saying that if I wanted his leg amputated, it had best be done. Limp had surrendered any judgment in the matter some time ago. So there was more to say.

"The Canberra boys," I said, "are smelling their way. They haven't cut out a wise policy, just a handy patch or two. Art of the possible, and all that. They should be — if they've got any — far deeper in their consciences than you. But maybe — "

"Go on," he said, with more satisfaction.

"I was just gonna say that maybe a politician can't afford any conscience. Unless he's in opposition."

"Too cynical."

"It's cynical, but maybe not too cynical. He's jam up against important decisions; bound to be. And he can't make perfect ones. Never. Look at the Head that expelled us. Leave me out of it. That Head knew very well that you didn't deserve expulsion, or he's a nitwit, a complete nitwit. Your entire school record was clean against it; and you would have been top of the year, too. But he was weak and I'll tell you what. He never could have practiced conscience and proper judgment before, with his staff and council. So when the council raged, and with the governor involved, he didn't come out with all there was to say for you. It was the same with Martin. Never said peep. Honesty has to be kept in play like a tennis ball, I bet. So when you come hard up against a hard imperfect decision, you make it, and it's still imperfect, but you can hold your head up. Honesty's in your way. You don't need to dog yourself daily with blame."

"I mightn't, either," Limp said, "if I could walk away from my decision not to register. If I could leave it and go on with my life."

"P'raps that's why I must register," I said, "and only why. It's not that I feel duty bound, or any patriotic fiddle-faddle. Damned if I'll be patriotic about bad things. But I wouldn't be able to extricate myself, either. I know this."

Limp groaned.

"You remember, Limp," I said, "how they used to recite those nauseating lines on Anzac Day? 'They shall grow not old.' That's vile claptrap," I said, "an insult to the dead.

"At the going down of the sun and in the morning
We will remember them.

132

"The sun goes down only once a year then. Who remembered them this morning? It gives poetry a pong," I said. "It's as bad as Pennyfeather. They're all Pennyfeathers!" I shouted, above the engine. "Poets, politicians, the lot."

"Who's he?" Limp said.

Now that he'd made me worse, he was beginning to feel better. So I had to tell him about Lew Pennyfeather and all. With a lieutenant colonel, retired, thrown in for good measure.

"For the love of Pete," I said, "is there anybody over twenty-five that isn't a bloody humbug, for God's sake?"

"It's all right for you," Limp said, "you can howl. You haven't got to register yet."

"Howl, howl, howl, like King Lear," I said. "He wasn't a humbug. Limp, when you get that form in Bellingen, bring two. And we'll take them up the mountain. We gotta think about this."

While he was in getting them, I was staring at the headlines on the newsstands, and because I'd been shouting and had stopped abruptly, I resented them with this terrific resentment. PACK RAPE and MURDER, they were telling each other, though the murder might have happened in Schenectady, Idaho, if Schenectady's in Idaho. On second thought, it's more likely to have happened in some feudal palace in Los Angeles, though the pack rape would be nearer hand. We can manage to brew it American enough. At any rate, I didn't think I would buy papers when I was older and was legislating for myself in a house of my own. They make every abnormality the normal thing, till you can't get by without blood in the imagination and sex on the nose.

Ah, well, Limp came back then.

"Bought this fruit," he said. "Better eat some."

"Limp," I said, "what we gotta understand is: the whole world's out to cop us. We gotta figure out some defense."

"The most peaceable defense," Limp said.

"Okay, okay."

That night, in Limp's lean-to, closed-in verandah, we were still agreed that the most peaceable thing was to register. But we disagreed when I said we should both do it.

"No," said Limp, "not having any. It's most peaceable to wait till you have to."

"Yes, but," I said, "you've gone beyond that. So we'll even it out."

"No," he said, "not having that. And if you pass the H.S.C. you can go on for years, for great hulking years. They'll defer you till you take your degree, and another degree after that, if you want to. That's peaceable."

"And the government may change, or the Act, or maybe there will just be peace on earth?" I said.

It was exactly what I'd wanted him to do, besides, and I told him so.

"Oh, but at that time," he said, "we'd been expelled, and I was pretty upset. Wanted to hurt myself as much as I could. Besides," he said, "I was tossing up about objecting. I'm quite sure I object."

"I object myself," I said, "to being made a monkey of by mere policies. I object, too. Of course I do. Following at the tail of great and powerful friends. When we've no sort of guarantee of what wildness will next issue from the White House. They don't represent us. And they're not much better at foreign policy than we are, and we've no redress for the steps they might take, or check or influence on them. Even if my own objections are as interested as Canberra's are, at least they're mine. Not borrowed off a driven President. And I've a right to my own convictions."

"Come back, come back," Limp was saying. "What do we do? Here?"

"Oh, we nurse our convictions in the quietness of our minds, like plenty others. Happen we'll go less wrong that way."

"Well?" Limp said.

"So I'm suggesting we do it together, that's all. I don't want to be gnawed at by doubt, for years and years, as to whether I'm my own master or not. Besides," I said, "I don't expect I'll pass the H.S.C. I'll need somewhere to go, I shouldn't wonder. Tell you what, we'll toss for it."

And I immediately tossed. "Heads I register, too." It was heads.

"Do it again," he said.

So we made it the best of five, and I still registered. So we made it the best of three fives, and on we went, and it only proved that tossing by lottery wasn't an adult proceeding. But then I said, "You see, Limp? We could tell them we've split the difference. Split the difference of our ages. They'll fall for that. If anybody ever asks, that is. Wanted to go in together, since we were mates. They'll think it good-oh. No moral sense at all. So we — "

". . . Or get off together," Limp was saying. "Not just go in together, but get off together? Even better?"

"Yes," I said, "of course. Gives us two chances of that, too."

So we laughed. "But it's all crap," he said. It brightened him, though, and we slept on it. In time we filled in and signed both forms, and put our birthdays on the same day late in the next six months, to make me older. To make us both older.

A day or two later, making my way back home, I didn't look at the view much. You don't, when you feel your country's about to make one of those *morituri* of you, that you're the sport of old men, not too responsible, that you wouldn't trust with your friendship, far less your life.

We weren't handing in any registration forms till the advertised date came, anyway. It would come soon enough. And I didn't want to take my form home. Wanted to wash my hands of it as far as I could, in a fatalistic way. Maybe it would all roll away, and we'd have a little prize in our hands, saying, *You have our leave to live your lives.*

But I kept saying to myself, *You shouldn't tamper, you shouldn't tamper.*

Well, I hadn't done anything at all. It might be the best of many bad courses. I had to take some bad course. It wasn't at all like going to the dentist's. You faced that. The dentist didn't ever say: *I'll take you and you and you. The rest of you can go home. And as for you two, I'm hauling all your bloody teeth out, no arguing. And my reason is, somebody's got to have false teeth.*

21

As if there weren't disturbances enough, the letter came from the Department and I hadn't passed. Hadn't passed the H.S.C. Of course, they don't say you've failed now. They tell you you've passed in this and that, but if you haven't matriculated, who could give a damn? It's this rank stink of suck-act that's so squeamishly contemptible. Kidding themselves, that's all. Kidding themselves with some theory or other. Didn't they know that I sat the H.S.C. to pass it, not to get some sense of achievement in metalwork or something? Somehow or other the world's taking leave of common sense and educationists are getting the upper hand of teachers. Another victory for incompetence, that.

And if you want to make your exams difficult, just don't make them bristle with extraneous difficulties, that's all. It's not that I want you to have no policemen lying in wait when next I sit an examination. There's more to it, though I was only on the edge of it that time. The threat of being called up is a serious threat to a young man. You needn't expect him to

137

study the better for it, or just forget about it as you do. He knows it's there, and it's not a fixed thing. It's very very iffy. For all he knows, he might just be grappling with a barrowload of smoke, and he hopes and hopes he is, day after day — when his mind could be growing otherwise. Anybody can get used to the fact that he has his conscription to do, automatically, like every other citizen. That won't buck him any more than compulsory voting after he's twenty-one. Far less, in fact. And he might even agree with a conscripted readiness. I do. But that's not how it is.

He knows that the government only needs some, and one way or other it's all the government will take. Did you ever see any better assurance of this than the medical? If he's caught on the lottery, there's still a 44 per cent chance of rejection at the medical. The Minister said it. Forty-four per cent rejected. Is it possible for anybody to believe, in the healthiest century, and by simple observation, that 44 per cent of twenty-year-olds are unfit for army service? There's no stand-to, that's all. And politically indifferent johnnies, a few, just a few, twenty-year-olds, have got to suffer the pretense that there is, because America escalated. There's a crisis there all right, and it sure will spread to us. But in any crisis there's a big, big element of timing. You've got to see and identify and prepare for the real crux. We can't boss a square yard of Asia with guns. The real crux is direct attack on our own difficult shores. Which men like ourselves turned their backs on for thousands and thousands of years, as they turned their backs on the tops of the mountains. We're the Swiss of the South Seas, behind oceans and deserts and outlying ways as they are behind their mountain redoubt.

And even if we're not, don't let us be so crass in our arrogance. How can we suppose that our flimsy culture can intervene in Asia, hoary with time, with traditions of which we've no understanding, not an inkling? I'm writing from Asia now, addressing you out of the edge of it. At this distance you ought to listen to me. I've got out of my adolescence, but have you?

Of course, I hadn't got out of it when the Department's letter came. I took it back to my bedroom to open it in private. It was early morning, but Mum rustled everybody up, and when I got in with my crestfallen face there was Mum fussing for support and protection behind Dad in his easy chair, and John barely in another chair, scratching head down, with his mouth full of sleep, and Robin with her sawn-off shortie pajamas in the other doorway. I could have wailed for them all. What a wetted disappointment I was to them.

John had stopped yawning, though he had a right to yawn. He'd already passed his year with two distinctions. Here I'd missed it only by one, but I'd missed it.

"Tell you what," I said, out of my agony, "I'm going to sit the February matric and I'll pass it. Sorry, everybody, I'm sorry."

So I had a January of swotting. Of course, I did get something out of it, and some fun, too. You can't be fearing the worst all the time. First of all, it involved a bit of sacrifice — of the whole of Angela, for instance. One Saturday, for a break, I went up to tennis not feeling very like it, and when Angela saw me, she said, "Guth, I'd like you to meet Sandy McNab. You can see he's every inch a Scotsman."

He was, too. I could see it. Not very tall, in tufts all over him. His hair was carroty red and curly and his figure was square to match. A great deal of low-set brawn, as if he'd sunk into the lower half of him. He was wearing slacks, or I bet his knees would have been white, and knobbly as the jowls of a Scots comedian. Those old inelegant plus-fours would have suited him now. His mouth was big and you couldn't see any teeth behind it — much like a shark's mouth, which looks unintelligent first of all when you meet it. But cheerful, he was cheerful — cheerful like he'd just won the shot-put at the Braemar Games.

"It's one up on me, Angela," I said, pretty mournful, feeling the weight of my study. "Can he play tennis, too?"

"How d'you mean *too?*" said Angela, in this high, orgiastic, surprised voice. Angela, I must say, always tended to be very hugely amused in one direction. Very tickled she was. But I was only thinking of the Braemar Games and the shot-put.

I had asked Dad to help me with my English and history again. He was resigned to it, but first of all he asked me in return, "What about Tech? Or Cram School, if it's shut?"

"Well, you see, Dad, to be perfectly honest, the classes are big, not personal, and the lecturer's only turning a penny. Besides, it's teaching, not lecturing, that you need for examinations."

"All right," Dad said, accepting this at once. But he

nodded with fierce menace, cutting the air with his eye. "You'll do me a written exercise twice a week without fail?"

"Yes," I said, "I'll be glad to."

And I was glad to. It could still be hell's delight going over those exercises. Took me two hours every time, and a great deal of roving about. Dad couldn't be bounded in a nutshell. He sure let you see there was a head of steam in teaching.

"English," Dad said, "is a wellspring. You must learn that it never runs dry; and then, quite frankly, I don't much care whether you pass your exam or not. But you'd better," he said, grimly.

So all that month I worked from morn to noon, from noon to dewy eve, the summer's day. The thing was: Dad's mind and mine were drinking together. It made thirst a joy. Literature, it's something to share, don't you know? That's of the essence of it. And but for the sharer, there's things you'd never see. For instance, it was Dad that showed me where the grief was in *Lycidas* — in the tug and dislocation of the lines —

> *Ay me, while thee the shores and sounding seas*
> *Wash far away . . .*

"And you hear it washing off the heart," Dad said, "for it reaches deep. And this man," Dad said, "knew more about the Iceberg Way of Writing than forty thousand Hemingways."

"How, Dad?"

"Well. For restraint there has to be a bloody horse. I'm not swearing, just quoting. Milton knew that you

141

had to rack and plumb and survey and map the Iceberg from end to end if you ever aimed to show it above water in writing. You couldn't just turn your back on it and keep downing a couple of quick ones with Jack Dempsey. Mostly restraint in Hemingway smacks of boredom and emptiness. It's a question of century, of course. Milton got as far as Job and the Psalms, and was content. You've got to see that the scriptures unfold and keep unfolding through history. Hemingway, he was at Ecclesiastes. Getting ready to be a thriving earthworm."

And while I was trying to get the hang of it, here was Dad saying in a thoroughly objectionable, minatory way:

> *Whatever the world thinks, he who hath not much meditated upon God, the human mind, and the Summum Bonum, may possibly make a thriving earthworm, but will certainly make a sorry patriot and a sorry statesman.*

All this sounded so like Dad that I've got him permanently tripped up with Bishop Berkeley now. They're still both right.

"You — don't like Hemingway, Dad?" I said.

"I will not believe in nothing."

Very peremptory Dad was, very, very peremptory. But it wasn't explaining, not even explaining himself. I'm quite sure we can't manage on nothing either, me and my buddies, or you and me.

22

THERE WAS JOHN, too; and Liz, who had passed the H.S.C., of course, and been suitably chagrined at my failure.

"And then, John," I said, "I'm thinking Liz might help me with the French and Latin."

"Bog me to death!" he said. "We're all nice and handy for you, aren't we? Lucky for us we didn't know anything of the ancient craft of greenkeeping, or we'd have been onto that lurk, too. We've just got to drop anything at any time and help you, have we?"

"Oh, well, John, even you don't collect your distinctions without some sort of lame assistance from the professors. And with H.S.C. being harder — "

"Harder?"

"I mean, John, you're doing what you want to do. I'm still having to spend my time on mathematics and things. Things that aren't any use to you after."

"Humph," said John. I could see I'd scored a point.

"And as I said, John, and it proves I'm serious, I'm going to hand you over Calpurnia tag, rag, and bobtail. For a whole month."

"Humph, but where's the car in the midst of all that? How do I know I'm not just getting some of your old clothes? It's a deal," he said.

I was amused at John, trying not to be a kid about it.

"Knew you'd come good," I said. "My, it's an awful help to me. Thanks, John. Just like you, old man. And I was serious about Calpurnia. A man can only be faithful to his ancestors, but he's got to pay his contemporaries."

That's how I persuaded John to look after my math as a bit of routine. After all, exams are a very mannered sort of a business. It's like eating peas or holding a wineglass. How can you know which way to do it unless you're shown? Every training needs a trainer.

So I said to John, "But you'll do me this last favor, will you? Just let me dash around in Calpurnia and put it all right with Liz, and I'll retreat to my bike from then on."

"Oh, that's how it is," John said. "Comin' a fast one on me, are you? Take it, but it'll be for the last time all right. You can peg away on your arteries after that."

I could see John was delighted. Saw himself whirling like Jehu into the hospital courtyard in holiday time with all the nurses up above at windows and balconies and hungry as a hundred Jezebels.

So I went looking for Liz. I took it slow, like the Dead March in *Saul*.

"Old girl," I said (to Calpurnia), "you're changing your boss for a bit. And he'll use the lash a bit more. He'll be less of a lover to you. But you can see

144

the necessity of it, can't you? No good behaving like a crocodile."

When I turned into Liz's street, there was another chariot bearing down against me and the first thing I noticed was a teen-age neckerchief capering in the wind like an army with banners. To see that always stirred me like the Marseillaise. Days of glory they were, and of a kind of Viking boastfulness, set up there at the wheel with flesh and beauty sitting feminine beside you, and you swam past in admiration of yourself. But this was Liz in the chariot!

We saw each other at the same moment. I was aware of Barry Blow presiding at the wheel and missing the moment completely, oblivious as a bargee bolting sausages and trundling along some stinking canal back home. But Liz put her hand to her mouth and looked in witty horror from me to Blow and back. Blow Blow, he doesn't even have a name you can kick. Unless for:

> Blow, Blow, thou winter wind!
> I'll kick your fat behind.

But that's going too far. You can only make a fool of yourself, making a fool of Shakespeare. Should be *thy* fat behind, in the first instance, and who would make a deity of Blow?

And I had to draw into the side. Liz and I were both going in one direction and looking in the other, as if our necks were wrung. It was encouraging when we were both doing it.

But I had to be quick, or they'd be around the corner. That Blow bloke was impervious to anything. So I hauled on the brake with a saw-edged sound, slapped my cheek with my palm, put my finger around my neckband, felt how I needed a shave, and all the time kept my elbow hull down on the horn.

And Liz waved as they vanished from sight. She'll have to explain that, I thought. Even a Blow-fly could see that. It looked a despairing sort of wave to me, as if Liz would be strapping on a life belt soon.

"And how did you explain to him, Liz," I said, "when you waved around the corner that time?"

It was the next day, a Sunday, and we were going through with a vote of censure.

"I didn't have to, really. I said, 'That was Mum,' before he asked."

Ever so sweet about it Liz was.

"You're a shocker, Liz, a real shocker. I was coming along to ask you to help me, too. To help with my French and Latin. And now I can't."

"Can't you? Why not? I can still help with your French and Latin, if you really mean to make a go of it."

"No, you can't," I said.

"Why ever not?"

"Why — not if you're going out with Barry Blow all the time." I was scandalized at the duplicity of it.

"I shan't be going out with him all the time," Liz said. "And what's it got to do with French and Latin?"

"But you just don't understand, Liz. Or, hell, you understand perfectly well. You're just being difficult. I'm not coming along to you because of damn French and Latin."

"Oh," Liz said, and her eyes were swimming about in

146

really classy Olympic pools. I could have dived in and shouted for joy —

"Oh," said Liz, "but you said you wanted help in French and Latin. Not that I'm much good, but I know you're worse."

"Look here, Liz," I said, "you're my girl friend in any language, and I'm not going to — Tell you what, I'll see the pants off Barry Blow. I nearly rammed you head-on yesterday, when I saw you in his bomb."

"And why didn't you?"

"Because you were in his bomb, of course. I wouldn't hurt you, Liz. Liz, the understanding is that you'll help me with my French and Latin, that I'll get through this exam like hell, that you and I must take to golf and bicycles, and one fine day

> *"In at the bathroom casement*
> *Windlesham bells shall call*
> *Liz and me, as the organ*
> *Thunders over them all.*

"Oh, I forgot

> *"Licensed now for embracement.*

"What a thing to leave out! Eh, Liz?"

"You're a madman," Liz said. "But it sounds good."

"And it'll *be* good," I said. "Liz, I've had to give Calpurnia to John."

I explained it all and Liz kept her misgivings to herself.

"All right," she said, "it's on. But who's holding the end of the lead?"

147

"What d'you mean, Liz?"

"I mean, you're trying to tell me what I can do and not do about Barry Blow, and I'm trying to tell you what you can do and not do about French and Latin. Is it fair, do you think? A clean swap?"

"Oh, no, Liz, it isn't. It isn't do and not do about Barry Blow. It's just not do."

"He's a nice boy," Liz said.

It might have gone on for a long time and it was most delicious poison. But, "Liz," I said, "come out with me tonight?"

"Where shall we go? It's Sunday."

"We'll — Well, let's take our bikes this afternoon instead and have a picnic at — "

"Dural," Liz said. "I know a place."

So we did that.

23

BUT THE GRAVER WORLD was hurrying me along. I passed
the matric in February and did well in English, so that
they were willing to accept me at the university, and I
was glad to go. Everybody at home was very pleased
and all the conversation was of happy days ahead.

"But I'm thinking," I said once, "that if I had to be
called up, I might go and do my two years first."

Robin was disgusted, John thought me crazy, and
Mum said, "This is so bad for my digestion, talk like
this at dinner."

But Dad asked me why.

"Because," I said, "when you read English and history, you need some experience of your own — especially for English, seemingly. All this time, Dad, you've
been showing it to me. I've felt so callow alongside
you."

Dad, of course, had been teaching better than he
knew, which is always what a good teacher helplessly
does. He can't help himself, I mean. Dad had even
told me, for the good teacher knows this very well. It
was what Dad called his humble knowledge.

"You must have met the man," he said, "who declares to his class with every word and gesture that he means to teach every one of them, before forty minutes are up, this and this and such and such limited things. Vanity," Dad said. "He's only a tinkling cymbal. Ought to have been a conjurer," Dad said. "Charlatan, that's what. Oddly enough, you won't meet much of it at the university. At least I hope not."

Dad's university had been over the sea.

"Why not, Dad?"

"I think it must be that they're more intelligent, for one thing, and therefore are fully aware of the difficulty of making any knowledge your own, far less anybody else's. And then the hungry sheep are older," Dad said. "You can't deceive older students with claims of teaching everything. Or even anything. What you do is urge them to teach themselves. They're winning things into their own judgments.

"Yes," he said, sadly, that night at dinner, "for literature there has to be maturity, that's true. It's really a *sine qua non.*

"Felix qui potuit rerum cognoscere causas."

Which we all thought a bit much to swallow with our meat, and the women protested out loud. But Dad went on.

"Poetry's sad, isn't it? It's just that," he said abruptly, "it's just that — the touch of real experience, it's always so devastating, too."

And he looked at me. He was hearing the noise of greedy Acheron in Virgil's lines. He showed me after, pretending they had no connection with me, that their relevance was broken, was for others. He didn't say any more at dinner, except that he was more inclined to corner the salt and had to say "sorry" quite often. Robin would have withered him with her long glances, but she had to ease them off ruefully on Mum, or make a face at me, as the cause of it all. Which I was, I was.

Liz knew, of course, that I'd been to see Limp, but I'd only told her that Limp meant to register next time and she thought it the wisest thing to do. I knew she wouldn't think it wise that my form was made out, too, so I didn't tell her. If I'd told my folks and Liz at that time, they would have compelled me to get it and tear it up. Beforehand, they would have had unanswerable objections. So I didn't tell them then. Kept thinking and thinking about it, especially in the night.

I knew it was a strengthener to Limp, and I knew beyond all doubt that the two years, if they were prosperous, would add immensely to my grasp and sheer enjoyment of letters. To do literature callow is to go off at half cock. I was able to see this, as I've said, because I had Dad's performance beside me. Not that I agreed with all he said, but that was (mainly) callow, too.

And there was one other thing. At school, in Cadets, I'd noticed this: that as soon as boys donned the uniform and stood out there in ranks, or assembled Bren guns, or whatever — as soon as they did this they became totally insensitive. A sensitive soldier was not a possibility. It was a consideration that drove young men into the R.A.A.F., but then you had to enlist for four years, with a short service commission, after your degree. I knew that, if ever I were a soldier, I would be a sensitive one, and that it would be lonely. I knew Limp would be sensitive, too. Best to be together, and admit to hesitations and gentleness now and then.

It isn't that I think all soldiers are Yahoos. Just that there was the tang of the barracks about their ways and virtues. The life of the barracks I had found, secretly, to be nasty, brutish, and mercifully short. You had to be a man, my son; you put a face on every clumsiness, and *bêtise*. I remembered a story of Dad's. In the Second World War, when he and some other rookies were called up, they were packed into a big icebox of a Methodist Hall in January in England, to sleep if they could. Dad had pajamas in his kit, but he didn't dare take them out. Stood and stared around the bunks. Finally went to bed in his shirttail. The sheer act of putting on pajamas when at war, or going to the wars, desecrated the manly code. He managed to tell some other men of this next day, to find that they'd done the same.

And then there was something that Angela said that I didn't agree with. I know, I have to be sure, that all soldiers aren't Yahoos.

"Oh," Angela said, "they haven't any consciences about it. I know plenty of boys that've been called up, and they just didn't think anything about it. They loved the army. Not to would be soppy."

At that time I said nothing, nothing at all. That last remark was a clue, but there was too little sense in what Angela said. All Angela meant was that she cared so little about anybody else that she couldn't ever divine what was going on inside them. She wasn't sensitive in the head. Her boys weren't likely to open their minds to Angela. Or to have minds in her presence? So I went home and thought about it.

Any boy, who had any head at all, was bound to have stirrings of conscience about this. If the country thinks otherwise, then the country is wrong. Young men, conscripted for two years, are acting against their own lives and interest, and this they are entirely aware of. They see their pals continuing as is. So they feel no call on themselves, only the force of a vagary conscription. They put down their reluctance to a natural timidity and think they'd better show courage, that it's all fair, that it'll come right. They would do this anyway, if only to forestall imputation and scorn from those that don't have to go. They soon know perfectly well that their fellow victims aren't likely to scorn them for their reluctance. But in spite of everything they think that they are the only despairers. So conscience is suppressed. It has been taken out of their hands and put in the hands of the state. Their fears and shame and embarrassment make them collaborate in the process. But the state can't possibly keep their consciences. And if by objecting they insist on having any, they will have to prove it. Justice is reversed for them. They will be deemed guilty and have the onus of proving themselves innocent. It's a complicated imposition on them, and few give it a thought. Judges must see it very well; it's brought under their noses; but they aren't paid to point it out. A judge's wisdom is commonly worldly-wise.

It isn't any wonder that young folk (like other folk) prefer to struggle quietly with their consciences themselves.

In February, Limp phoned.

"Here," he said, "I gotta register now, you know, this month. Thanks for getting me used to the idea. I was wondering . . . Your form? Shall I tear it up?"

"No," I said, "please send it in."

Oh, well, even if we were drawn and had to go, maybe even then they wouldn't send us out of the country. Some soldiers always stay at home.

24

WE WERE DRAWN, TOO. We didn't escape. I was faced with the problem of telling people about it. Fortunately or not, John brought the mail in that day, and he came straight to my room. It was after Easter. Time had dragged on.

"Hi," he said, "here's a letter from the Department of Labour and National Service. And it's for you."

I just grabbed it from his hand, poor John. Tore it open, but after I'd read it I gave it back to him silently, sat up in bed, thought of a few things, like going to the loo. John had sunk down on my desk chair, with his elbow among my books and essays, and, because of his concern, I cordially let him do that.

"You're gonna be called up?" he said.

"Might be, too."

"But you're only just nineteen. Shouldn't have registered."

"But I did, though."

"Mum know about this?"

"No," I said. "Look, John, I'll have to go for a leak. It's important. Keep it under your hat."

"Ass," he said.

John hadn't called me a single crude word till then, and I was obliged to him.

"Oh, well," he was saying, as I retired, "he'll get deferred. But why the hell did he do it? *Vision and Rhetoric, Articulate Energy, Science and the Shabby Curate of Poetry,* by Martin Green: what the hell sort of a study's that? Where's the use of it?"

I stood in the doorway, listening till he was done, and then I went in and leaned on the towel rail, and smiled. Funny man, John. I'd have to get in touch with Limp. All the birthdays on the dates balloted were called up. But it could be that after all he'd given us different birthdays? Anybody that bothered to look at us could see we weren't born on the same day. Maybe he would have reasoned that different dates gave more chance for one of us to get off? With gambling, you can't ever tell what a fellow will finally do, can you? Look at horse racing. Some folks bite off all their nails, or beat their wives, or go and shoot themselves. There was just a dog's chance. If he'd invented separate birthdays for us, then he could be in the clear, and I could get deferred to finish my degree. I wasn't bursting to be in the army.

I took Liz to Uni, not John. She had the same classes mostly, and it was very agreeable to have her beside me. I drove with less fatigue. Besides, the arrangement was on a perfectly proper, sound and financial basis, or she wouldn't have come.

"What's wrong with you today?"

Liz had on a new outfit and I hadn't mentioned it yet, I suppose.

"Well, I prefer mini-skirts," I said. "You must know that?"

"Oh, yes," Liz said, "of course I know that." Liz was merry about it. "We've just got to disappoint you now and then," she said.

It was some kind of medieval crimson tabard with flowing Chinese trousers of a perfectly heavenly black. An ensemble, featuring her lipstick. Togetherness it was.

"But I like it, Liz. I'm not disappointed at all, I like it a lot. Very chic."

"Oh, don't go on. Conning me. It's too late now. Shut up, will you. And watch where you're going." She sighed herself back into sadness. "There's something bothering you, I know."

"But, Liz," I said, "I like anything with you inside, you know that?"

I smiled on Liz, but it didn't bring an answering smile.

"Liz, I'm caught in the call-up and I'll tell you about it."

"No," Liz said, and flatly refused to believe it. Liz had both hands flat on her thighs in a ready-steady-go way. Made me feel better at once, because I envied them. We had to park in a place we knew, and miss a lecture, and cuddle pretty fast, and admire the view of the city, before we got anything like adjusted at all.

I had to say, after I'd explained it twice, "But, Liz, I don't see why you should be so outraged! It's the very God-damned thing I'd have to do a year hence anyway."

"Who runs to meet these things? Like that?"

Liz wasn't old enough for tears, so she didn't weep

any, that I noticed. Or didn't share them with me, maybe. She retreated over my shoulder more than once, and clung, and her hankie was crushed in her hand, and she blew her nose. But when I said, "Dear Liz," she said, "Let's go on. We'd better. Please let's go to Uni, Ian."

And I had to, because it was an unconditional admission.

I think she fiddled in her bag for an Aspro, but she denied it, when I said there was a packet in the glove box. She didn't want to talk. Poor Liz. Girls can build a little world around a boy friend, and if it comes to nothing, they're the wounded soldiers, nearly always. And I know why. It's because they're more generous than boys, and sooner surrender to the love of one man. I hope Liz will be happy in her life, with or without me.

After a long time — three minutes? five minutes? I had to say again, "What I notice, though, is that everybody's going to be appalled and stupefied and nonplused when the very same thing . . . Why should it be more hellish at nineteen than twenty? Why am I ripe and expendable by then?"

But Liz probably didn't think me ripe and expendable for a year or two yet. She wouldn't answer. You attack the wrong person, very often, when you're indignant about anything. I could make no headway. The whole of society, and Liz with it, has strained itself to get used to one outrageousness at one time only. If you're twenty, it's in the rules. If you're nineteen, it's inexplicable. It's the same bloody evil at either age, I say. Pick us all, or give over picking. I'm not defending being called up, but I'm prepared to be called up for three to six months, or a year if you can pay for it, to be in a readiness with everybody else, and show it.

But not to put Asia right by force. You do it if you're able; it's beyond me, and France has given up, and Britain, and the Dutch, and so will the United States, and surely to God we see that they've had to? And so will Russia, if you have patience. You don't beat the East. And I'll tell you another thing if you leave it alone: it fights its wars with itself. You don't think South America's my business, and it's hellish enough to want a bit of straightening. Oh, no, I'm not the zealot here. Meddle for yourself, that's all I'm saying.

Limp phoned in the evening, and he hadn't changed his birthday.

That's enough.

25

<hr/>

THAT SATURDAY NIGHT, after football, I thought I might as well show up at Jimmy's, because there was likely to be a very great silence in our house, with me at the center of it. Everybody was behaving too badly to go on about it, and anyhow this isn't a family chronicle.

I'd been going to football practices and a mate of John's who was in the First Fifteen soon said to me, "You carry on as you're doing, Guthrie, and you'll be in the First Fifteen in no time."

From a seasoned player, this was praise. You could say he was the best player on the team, too. Fullback, magnificent kick, thunderest tackle, and the loudest voice heard on the football committee in years. He was called O.B., on account of his first two initials, but if you didn't admire him much you called him Ob, though never to his face. You didn't even allude to his first name, which was Olaf. People said it was Olaf if you asked them, and I couldn't think of any other name beginning with O that you'd have to keep dark. He practically picked the team, collected subs, spent them, said who qualified for Blues, did everything. I tell you it was something to be told to carry on by O.B.

There was one thing else you had to do. You had to go to Jimmy's on Saturday nights and get squiffed. Once you had a sure place you didn't need to, but until that time it was wise to be there. You could stick your hand down your throat and puke in the urinals later if you liked. It was too disgusting for anybody to object openly to that.

So I went that Saturday night. Might as well get used to a he-man's world. And look around while I had the chance, to see how they lived it up, and what sort of civilized city-types I'd soon be fighting for.

"Ah, there's young Guthrie," said O.B. "Young Guthrie, we'll make a place for you down there." He pointed, so there could be no mistake. "Where's your brother? Swotting like hell, I suppose. Give him a middy, Jim. Shandy, first go off, till we see how he does. I'm answerable to the mothers of these coons."

Jim didn't say anything, just looked used to it.

"Know Bloody Pestle yet?"

"Who's Bloody Pestle?"

"Professor of thermonuclear dynamics." He said it as though he'd just given birth to the Chair, as perhaps he had. O.B., the actor, always had an anguished look. "We're just going over him here. He's always trotting out the bull about how ignorant the nonscientists are. Seems to believe it, too."

O.B. turned his back to the bar and leaned on it with his elbows. He tilted his gaze at the cornice of the wall opposite. O.B. never looked you straight in the eye. His eyes would flutter, vanish into the top of his head, change places with his tonsils. All the time his upper

161

lip would be quivering distended over his exposed gum. This was O.B.'s affability. It was another thing you didn't speak of.

He'd had his nose broken once, and it made his face very craggy. He had high Viking cheekbones and very black hair, long, plastered down, shiny like Adonis sweating from the chase. The shape of O.B.'s head was most noble, with the bump at the back that goes with nobility. When he was in process of flattening an opponent on the football field, there was no sign of hesitation about him. His voice was always a shade too loud, and full of himself. His chief buddy, a charlatan who'd never played a game of football in his life, kept pointing out how he had the biggest jake known to research since the fellow built in with the ruins at Pompeii, that the guides will show you, in hope of extra cash. O.B. was silent about this accomplishment of his, but his silence spoke complacency. The smile on the face of the tiger. Once he grew a pimple on it. I just forget exactly where, but it was king-size, too. He was just as big in the head. Had taken some degree or other, and was doing a second one, probably divinity.

"It's the custom," O.B. was saying, "to tender a little salutary advice to First Years when they graduate to Jimmy's every Easter. To each according to his need."

"Ho, everyone that thirsteth," Peters said, walking about and making as if he tolled a bell, "here he comes. Stand by for an important announcement. Calling all cars, calling all cars."

Listening to Peters, I began to think you just said

anything at Jimmy's — to prove you could talk. Or else he was damned drunk.

But O.B. carried on, dipping his lids to the cornice.

"In winter," he said, "always wear flannel next the skin. I've never done it, but it's what I was told when I came up and I've never doubted its wisdom. One believes the Commandments without following them all that much. So I pass it on officially, honoring the ancestors."

"Trouble is," Peters said, pacing about like a zoological exhibit, "it's a thing the women don't approve, man. You'd better tell them you don't advise it for wenching."

"It's said now, it's immutable. Besides, I'm not advising wenching for them yet."

O.B. unhooked his eyes from the ceiling, focused them to avoid seeing anything near at hand, but he couldn't sustain it. Had to take flight for the ceiling again. The three or four First Years were hanging like bees from his lips. It gratified and it embarrassed him. He might even have known his utterance was hollow as the Delphic oracle or the voice of some TV strong man, advertising. After all, he was a clever bastard. Too clever to fill the air every Saturday night with nothing but this wind and piss. He salvaged himself from his lean, and his eyes and his eyelids and lips went all coloratura again, and he clutched at his schooner like a kid grabbing its mum's skirts, and he downed his mouthful of ale. Only a mouthful, and what a time he took at it.

I could see this O.B. was acting too big a part, like the frog that burst into bits. O.B. was the usual ego-

163

centric political big shot, leading blokes along a road they were already going. Much of the way he hated it. But he liked leading.

He got back to his elbow on the bar, without ever taking his eyes off the cornice while his balance swayed like a gyroscope. Compensation. Proved he could look the cornice in the eye, if it ever would grow one. Except for the First Years, and Peters, the rest of the football crowd were talking gravely among themselves. Another part of the act.

"Next," said O.B., "I want you to abjure the company of women. Brothels are out, unless maybe twice a week. It's bad for your studies and even worse for your football. I don't say I object to the sight of a skirt on the touchline of a Saturday afternoon. We all play the better for it. But nothing more, positively nothing. Unless for the Saturday hop, every fortnight, in the Union, eight P.M., a dollar a couple.

"And the precincts of the Women's Hostel till eleven fifty-five precisely, precisely, boys. Love is no more than a matter of *perfect* timing, you can take it from me, of *perfect* timing, I say again. Take it to your hearts, note it well. It is given gratis, it is given gratis."

Gee, for innuendo now, give Peters a bit of chalk and a blackboard and I believe he'd have written it all up, in case we missed any. As it was, he paused demurely and fixed us through his shaggy-dog eyebrows, then giggled like an old man in shorts and T-shirt. At least he was a relief to O.B. with his fullback's heavy irony. We First Years were all taking it like sour plums we'd stolen, because we were all abject crawlers for places in O.B.'s bloody football teams. Mums used to say when she was happy, "The things we do for England . . ." and I can see what she meant now. I'd sooner have told the philosophy professor to stow the junk he was talking. I'd sooner have told the vice chancellor where he got off. And for this reason: the vice chancellor has a permanent appointment, whatever anybody says. He can afford to be magnanimous. But not O.B. O.B.'s place was just piracy on the high seas. Any contradiction was the black spot, to be hurled back at compound interest.

"Thirdly," said O.B., "about drinking." They always tell you about that, because it makes men of them. "Five gallons of beer a day is far too much in training. No more than three schooners daily after meals, if you wish to grow to be a man, uncompromised by a hobnailed liver. Myself, I would conscientiously recommend a little less. A firkin a fortnight is excellent alliteration. It's far too much beer.

"And you may go to lectures now and then," O.B. said, "with my blessing."

He paused. You could see there was another movement coming. It came gently, like little Lord Fauntleroy.

"And there's just one other thing, but I've delegated it to Peters. It wouldn't come quite gracefully from me. But I thought it out in the beginning."

Peters had the hide for anything. Last year when our boys won the Comp., Peters had turned up for the team photograph, flattened his abdomen on a table in the dressing room, said *Hello, boys,* and showed some extra teeth to his sheepshead grin, to compensate for what he was going to do. With O.B.'s backing. And there he is now, grinning in the photo, with his place in history.

And here was smarmy Peters tackling another smarmy job.

"You must all be aware, boys," said Peters, taking a deep breath and the center of the floor and talking to the whole bloody pub and grinning like a death's-head and holding his beer and his little finger in front of him, and genuflecting at this word "aware": like that, second syllable dropped about a fifth. I can't help it. He did all this. He even pulled up his pants with a jerk after, as though they were leaving him like the god Hercules whom Antony loved.

"You must all be *aware*, boys, how our esteemed fullback, the secretary of the University Football Club, O.B., on my right, out on Thursday, price nothing —"

Here Peters bobbed down his usual fifth or so, then extended his arm like the Statue of Liberty very near, then giggled and gobbled and expected the applause. Laid on like that, of course, it's bound to come. All the hams got it, and howled, and after all it was easy. O.B. had wangled a feature in *Alma*, the student paper, and there he was taking up practically the whole front page. There's a semblable coherence about everything. The editor hadn't really any choice. But Peters had resumed: " — has just accomplished his degree. You might wonder how come, with so busy a man. But he's done it, with First Class Honors, in classics, and the vice chancellor has clapped him on the shoulder and all. Didn't dare risk his head. *Great wits*, you know, and all the rest of it."

Peters giggled, salivated, shot a flattering glance at

O.B., and was so animated that his hair started curling around his ears.

" — And I'm proposing, boys, that we celebrate this auspicious occasion in a significant manner. As he says himself, very modestly, it isn't that it's likely to form a precedent. For who else in the football team will ever again take first-class honors in classics? I wouldn't have it in a gift, would you? So, with his blessing, and the committee's, I suggest we have a do on Saturday fortnight. Take a room somewhere, bring your molls, and it'll cost you no more than a smacker each. What say? And the drink extra, of course. The club's going to stand in for ten bucks, as a gesture of pride and dignity. And you won't have any trouble beforehand. It's all arranged, ready to press the button."

Well, you see, it was all a bit of pub-storming. How can you make a serious objection in a pub? Besides, nobody seemed to want to. It's odd how a crowd of fellows can hate the guts of a boss-guy like O.B. and still do everything he says. But if they didn't, they couldn't hate him any more, could they? What gets them is the way he has them spontaneously doing anything for his vainglory. They can't understand it. Think they're the only one that hates him like hell.

So that was how we all went home rejoicing in our matchless chief, and I was saying to myself: Well, if I go, I'm not taking Liz to that one. It'll have to be Angela.

And what a pair of vicarious bastards to be called up for! Not the girls, of course.

There was the meanness first of all. I felt pretty certain that O.B. and Peters, presiding over the collection

167

of the smackers, had no intention of putting in any smacker of their own. Only the saps would smack. There was simply one thing I would want to be less — less, I mean, than a sap paying out a smacker — and that was the bugger battening on it. But excuse me. You get so contemptuous of smarmy Peters and his kind, and big Jerusalem guys like O.B., that your contempt crowds out your vocabulary and leaves the hodmadods of Monomotapa, though a nasty people, gentlemen in their speech at least. I know I just didn't like those fixers.

And then there was their wit abounding. Guys like O.B. without a scrap of merriment in their natures, and they have to crap on and be the life of the party and make everybody laugh like Mephistopheles with hell-fire searing his guts. They're only saying what they've heard a whole line of Plantagenet boss-guys say before them. They confuse noise with personality and smugness with wit. So pleased with themselves that they have to be funny. And Peters's kind of clinging innuendo — faugh!

They were all singing when Angela and I got there a fortnight later, and I shammed I was clued up on all the songs. It's no good showing you're only learning half the time. You can't be tough that way.

Still, I didn't know them: "Frankie and Johnny," "The Foggy Dew," "Sing a Song of Sixpence" to the tune of "Adeste Fideles," with a mighty deviation at the end. Which took it right out of the nursery class and made it a student song. I'm not having anybody sing it to my kids, even when they're dead asleep. There's still automation, or Aldous Huxley or something, and it's too bloody risky. Earnest, attunable, then medically bawdy. We sang it nicely in harmony, had a real flair for the ironies, and it sounded very well with the pub going full blast. Sounds of cans clinking, beer slurping, lechery nibbling, patrons quietly chatting away at the pitch of their voices like they were all littlies again — given those things, and practically anybody can sing like the angel Gabriel.

At the pauses we encored the scandalous ones: The maid was in the garden, explaining to the groo-oo-oom . . . I suppose she would have to take the clothespin out of her mouth to explain? That would be the funny bit. Incongruity and all that. Anyway, it's how my mother explained to me, in similar circumstances. And I always took it as pleasant conversation, not funny at all. Strange how detached from the world you get when you're on a kiddie car.

Those words banged back and forth in the chaste male and female ears of all the patrons. Not to worry. It did them no harm. They were maybe too accustomed even to listen. I watched their half-cheerful faces, like a book of Dickens in eclipse. They were wondering what the hell had come over their pub. Students, just typical, they were thinking. Like a dog cocking his leg at a lamppost and so callow as to think that the lamppost had been put up for that. I helped them out with that last reflection, of course.

To be quite honest with you, if any citizen came in with a big smirk on his pan, I thought far less of him, even supposing he was tending to ooze tolerance and how he'd sacked cities in his own young day. At his age he should have known better, or at least been more ambivalent about it. But you can't expect grownups to be ambivalent, either. What the hell! Most of them haven't been thrown with a thought in years. To most of them a thought would be as antediluvian as a brontosaurus. Oh, no, in these gaudy leisured days of ours there's a hell of a lot of sheer lack of time for anything, especially thinking.

Most often, too, you could just shelter under the mere noise of it. Really, it was only terrible to people when we left out half a line, like a check stub. The silence till John Brown's Body was resurrected again was terrifically embarrassing if you were caught like the Bedouin gravely on the march to the bar counter. Especially if you'd a high hemline and a nylon frou-frou. It must have been like walking the plank — into a sea where all the sharks were of the opposite sex.

Personally, I thought it all a bit mad, chaps bawling like hell and smiling to each other about words I didn't perfectly catch. Guess I didn't know any better than the groom, though it's depressing to admit it.

Then the dancing came on, but by that time I'd found out, quite suddenly, that I'd drunk one too many and like a fool I struggled against it, when I should have gone and been sick. It was just discomfort, I thought, for I'd only had about four drinks and I was a big boy now. Just couldn't be sick.

"Aren't you dancing?" Angela's words sounded blank, apart. I tried to make my ears start singing.

"Course I'm dancing. What d'ya think? Might sit out and have a drink this round, though."

"My, what a man you've grown!"

But Angela was puzzled a little. Maybe she thought

170

I was sulking, or dreaming of my darling love of Liz. She would also have been spotting with an eye to business all the guys that would dance with her. And to give her credit, she wasn't an oozy-boozy woman at all. Didn't want to squander love with a can.

"How's Liz?" she said once, without much interest.

I said, "Fine," and conversation lapsed. She yawned once or twice. I was too miserable to care. I didn't explain my Plimsoll Line to her. I was sorry for the fine dress she had on and all the trouble she'd gone to — the hairdo, the pert little face pinched into disappointment already. But I didn't know how to cheer up the inside of me. I thought: Maybe a glass of beer? Maybe a blowtorch?

I was glad of the stir of it, and the horsiness of the boys, all returned from the day's great football matches and shimmering in the women's beauty, deserving the fair because they had been brave. In such a company I could rely on Angela to light upon some settled low content. Soon she went off with somebody — I can't remember who — while I sat there gazing into my pot of beer.

Somebody around my head was saying, "Scrofula — Bloody hell — Tomorrow — Oh, God, at Avalon — That picture — Abstract of the bridge — Can't you see? — He's soused already — Never heard of him — Expelled — Let's have a dance — Why shouldn't we?"

I put together in my head the scrofula and the bit about tomorrow, and I was far back at a Pictish landfall with night coming on and a standing-stone on the hill to the west at the edge of the pitch-black waste, and an assured voice lasting through those drooling voices:

Light thickens; and the crow
Makes wing to the rooky wood.

I saw Macbeth at the little shot window, with life gone harsh and bare. Ravens croaked the evening in at Bobbin Head, always, right back to the Stone Age. But Liz and I were new.

"Liz," I said, I shouted, "Liz, where are you?"

They hauled me into the urinals and I was very very sick. I'm glad they got me there, and I'm glad Liz didn't hear me then. I'm glad they didn't all come staring at me when I was put out on the verandah to air off. Girls' backs are usually nice, but not when they're righteous. I wish I could have explained something — that I wasn't soused, that I was going to be called up and leave them pretty soon. It was cold on that verandah.

I went in and fought to defend my body from the saxophone.

"Why don't you go home?" Angela said.

I can't say how long it was before she said it.

"What time is it?" I said.

I think I might only have been dozing off and fighting this saxophone with my drumming nails. I felt better.

"How've you bin, Angela?" I said. "Sorry I've kind of sabotaged this party for you."

"Oh, you haven't. Not at all. Don't apologize. I'm doing fine. It's a beaut party all right. Thanks for bringing me. That's all. Say, the boys are free-an'-easy all right, aren't they? You were right about that."

Angela could sound surprised about anything. And pepper you in a sauna bath of stinging little Finnish

sentences, too. I was just a little offended at her enthusiastic tone. What's wrong with you, Guthrie? I
thought. Don't be turning sensitive. I couldn't bear it.

Angela was saying, with her hands on her knees for
intimacy, "If we packed you nicely into Calpurnia, Ian,
do you think you could smell your way home?"

"Yes," I said, edging away from her. "Especially the
smelling. Who's we? I can take a hint, you know, Angela. No need to put it crudely at all."

"Oh, no, I know," Angela said, laughing, mistress of
herself, putting a hand up to finger her pearls. "No, but,
seriously, I think the best place for you tonight is bed.
You oughtn't — "

"Angela, I've always thought that. Is it a proposal or
anything? You've always thought it yourself, haven't
you, Angela? Where's this bed you're offering me? Us?"

For a minute Angela ducked like a bush in a cyclone;
then she said in wheedling good humor, "It's your own
bed, silly. And don't be rude. I'm — "

"Before you go any further, Angela," I said, "I'm due
for call-up now, and I don't want any more of this
mushy doghouse."

"You're drunk," said Angela.

"No," I said, "it's true. I just haven't been living in
your bosom lately, so how could you know? Happened
over a fortnight ago."

And I showed her the letter, which I carried about
with me, in case I wanted to tear it up at any time.
She let some offsider read it as well, and she gave him
a questioning look. Then she said, "Aren't you only
nineteen?"

"Yes. My folks have been telling me I am."

173

"You mean to say, Guthrie, you've registered a year too early and been taken?"

It was smarmy Peters, this offsider. Poked his way around the appointments of Angela and interrogated me. Smarmy bloody Peters.

"I don't mean to tell you anything," I said.

"But you have told me. Now. He must have been," he said to Angela. "He's a clever man, Guthrie. He must have been thinking that if he missed out, here was this card in his hand. He was free. And if he got caught, he could plead a mistake in his birthday and have another go next year. Two chances to beat the odds. Very clever."

I was on my feet, and swaying dangerously, and angry. Actually, what he had said had gone through my mind, though I never had the least idea of trying it. Dad had toyed with it, too.

"Thatsh not it. Punch your bleedin' head in."

"Oh, then a martyr, a martyr, must be a noble martyr." Peters giggled.

"Let me — "

But Angela got up and tried to make me sit down again and in her embraces I forgot for the time about Smarmy. Thought I was a black bear, discovering a hive of honey, and grunting in my glee. Then Angela got me down and in my mind I went over the clutching, very pleased.

Peters sounded his hunting horn of a giggle as he held out his hand and confidently took Angela's hand. I could see his signature tune poking right out of his head. *Thank you for giving me* — I'm not going on with it. Lascivious innuendo. Peters had a mutton-chop attitude to sex. But it was a mutton chop that had already been hoarded too long, and had gone stale on him, really.

I wasn't having him insinuating any motives into my actions. It's one thing thinking a thing for yourself. It's quite another, though, if Peters thinks the very same thing. And I was astonished. Here was one insight that sobered me, and suddenly I got up and drove straight home.

There's something physical about learning. Vaguely I'd known before that actions weren't decisive of themselves, but how you approached them. Even if I'd pleaded that I was too young to be called up (and they wouldn't gainsay it, however they might treat me), still my pleading would have been quite free of the obliquities that Peters imputed to me. I wasn't trying to avoid honest dealing, but to go through with it in this impasse.

It's meaningless, too, just to know at a distance that thousands are in death and misery in Vietnam. You don't do anything to stop your part of it. Because you don't really know it. It isn't a part of you.

When I got into Calpurnia, though, and started her up, there was another thing to think about. *Hey,* I said to myself, *the breathalyzer, what about that?* And I switched Calpurnia off again, to let her think it over quietly.

But I'm not drunk, I said. *I can think about everything quite clearly and capaciously. Can see to the bottom of Angela and the bottom of Peters, as well. Futtrick, they're all punk, no-hopers completely. And here's a chance,* I said, *if your blood should still be drunk, a chance to get clean off. Ram the boot of some other silly bugger and push him head-on into a passing taxi — because taxis are always belting too fast, anyway. They'll cop you then, all right. And clap you in jail, and maybe for life, and you won't have to bother about your responsibilities anymore, not ever again. For the army won't have you unless you're as pure as the naked heavens. It likes something it can spoil. Rob a bank, and your conscription's over. Well, how about that, Calpurnia? Just how about that?*

I could see Calpurnia thought it wasn't on, not at all. And neither did I think it was on. I'm just as responsible as they come at twenty, and I hope you've noticed. If all the old duty-bound bastards, the pundits, constipated with their seriousness, were as tenderly responsible as me, I wouldn't be drunk, conscripted, or writing any of this. Real peaceable my life would be.

So I said to Calpurnia, "Let's go home, old girl. Slowly and decently. And to hell with them."

I sang sometimes, loudly and out of tune, to set on edge the teeth of the world. And I bawled out at one or two passing vehicles, too.

Don' wanna go. Not any more 'n you. Why should I? Home you go, go home and sleep in your beds. Don't give us a thought, will you, we're only the *morituri, morituri,* that's all we are. Butchered to make a Roman holiday. To give you a night out every Saturday. But you needn't think of us poor lads lost in the ground.

And they didn't. I'm sure they didn't. Generally, they were a mile or two farther back before I got all of that said. But I knew what I was doing all right, I knew it well. I was motoring into the darkness.

176

26

I WOULD, as I was already well aware before I joined it, always abominate any army. A master at school once turned and charged me, "Guthrie, you're against all forms of regimentation, are you?"

The phrasing of the question, and his amused face, both of which I've stored away in his praise, make him an understanding man, to my kind. He was inclined to envy and encourage me in this recalcitrance. For we're more like ants than we think. We regiment — we regiment education and commuting and the herding of men in cities till everything shrinks to a sameness. And neither we nor the ants could have advanced in our societies without it, I know. But it's drab, drab for the individual, who becomes just that instead of a man, becomes an individual.

There was a streak in my ancestry that tended into suffering as a reply. It came from Dad's side. At a guess, Dad had been hit more than once in his life, and had immediately, even proudly, stepped aside, elected out. There must have been a snail somewhere in the Guthrie forefathers. But there was also a bear, for Dad had his revenge all right. He persecuted his own family with his Ezekiel sallies and Jeremiah threatenings. How doth the city sit solitary that was so full of people, he would cry, for no reason at all, and he was seeing and foreseeing the emptiness at the heart of it, that everything would become as Central Station at two in the morning, a windy waste of ugly platforms and rails swooping away to nowhere.

It wasn't that the Guthries were too proud to be ordered about, not at all: they could lay the lowliest duties on themselves and cheerfully help poor people. The reason for the hatred of regimentation and consequently of armies is very easy to isolate. It lay in the value they put on imagination. Regimentation is the Grand Inquisitor of that. It wasn't simply the lack of freedom. Undeviating service of poetry or God or science is to many a man a perfect freedom. But to be chided in his imagination all the time is a hell of suffering to the man who lives by it, and must live by it. There are such men, for I was such a man. Right turn, About turn, Stand at ease, meant that I had repudiated ease for servitude, not service. Indeed, in our first days in the army, a captain who understood those things as a Boy Scout might, exulted over us in the ranks and said that the army had us twenty-four hours a day, that we lived and breathed the army. This isn't only how it is, but how it has to be, and it's damnably opposed to the spirit of man, the very thing that it contradictorily maintains.

"You haven't shaved this morning!"

The R.S.M. was an inch from my face and bawling. Most soldiers in this perilous strait say nothing and try not to shit themselves, or so they tell you after. But I had shaved.

"Haven't shaved this morning!"

"Yes, sir."

"You haven't shaved."

"Yes, sir."

He looked me up and down and a silence fell on the continent of Australia.

"Must've took two steps backward from the razor then."

The R.S.M. careered around the rest of the ranks and the sergeant had to run to keep up, but my smile was still standing to attention and staring hard into the east.

That was my earliest gleam of hope. It wasn't that it taught me to shave more carefully, though it did. That R.S.M. was called Rob Roy, and his chin jutted like the charge of the Highlanders at Quebec. We had all expected some fearful depredation, because the sergeants and corporals were listening for interest and instruction on how to brook these matters, and the prestige of rank was involved. It was the R.S.M that set these things aside and managed to extricate the pair of us. I saw with admiration as well as gratitude that his imagination had been ruined to some purpose. He was a leader of men, and it was the very army that had saved him from a life of laboring.

"What made you do it?" some silly bastard asked at tiffin time. "What made you contradict him?"

"But," said Limp, "he had shaved. I saw him."

"Yes, but an extra two days of jankers — "

"I had bloody well shaved," I said.

"Yes, I know — "

179

"Look," I said, "I couldn't have him making a mistake. He's a respectable man."

The only thing I liked was map reading. It's significant, but hardly any regular soldier does, under the rank of major. I think it's because there's nothing in the issue of kit before an officer's coat that has a comfortable inside pocket for holding a map, or even a printed book. Think of the joys of that. Of course, this laggardness in map reading doesn't mean that any battles are lost. As long as busy-topped trees are recognizable and not too close together, any platoon will be able to lay down a field of fire and the shrapnel will correct inaccuracy. A truck driver can ask his way, or if not, the enemy will tell him.

But when you're a recruit, a talent for maps can lead to sharp promotion right away. Very soon I was lecturing to all NCOs from the battalion far and near without number or exception (barring the staff sergeant that sent the order out) on contours, re-entrants, reference points, churches with towers and spires, churches without any towers and spires — the whole peaceable layout of the countryside. They felt they had to call me corporal, by gee. In the army experts proliferate and atonement is made. They respected me and thought I would be, like Enoch, translated to some suitable augustness. To them I was a lance corporal, acting, unpaid, and from experience they knew it to be a step forward, in irony, at least. But what's the use of going on about these matters?

The time came when I was on embarkation leave and Liz and I were always at the beach. It was the end of November, last November, and it went fast. All

that fortnight we swung on the edge of the ocean, because I wanted to, with its waves sounding and sounding. Sometimes the surf was eight feet high and you
couldn't see the horizon over it. Sometimes as the wave
hung breaking, like ours, the sun got in and lit it from
end to end, and caught in the long corridor of water
would be a fish, swimming in its own red blood in the
incorruptible sea-green. And then, as the day waned,
the blue of the open sea was the wine-dark afternoon
color that Odysseus sailed on, or the Trojan Aeneas.
And I was to sail on it.

We searched out places of our own, of course, because we'd come for each other, not for a swim or the
sun or the company. Except this company of sea and
sky, and time that laps you on every side and lends
some comfort because of it.

Not that Liz was disposed to be mute or easily com-
forted. She wouldn't talk about herself or her degrees
at all, showed some impatience with me if I alluded to
it.

"Oh, that, stow that. Suppose I'll soldier on as a
teacher some day. Or pilgrim it, too."

"How d'you mean *too*, Liz?"

It was Angela's old question. Liz stared me out,
shook her body off me and stared me out. Disheveled
feminine despair and protest was in every bit of her as
she leaned on one arm and leg, her hair hanging down
like Niobe's.

"You didn't need to leave that map reading," Liz
said, indignantly. "You volunteered for Vietnam."

And so I nodded and admired her, loved her very
much. We were still only twenty but Liz had always

been my girl friend and was likely to be, as far as I was concerned. I wanted her. But I also wove a charm around her, because I prized her — loved her, I know well enough. Poor Liz, there was little she could do to sort the present plight of things.

"Why did you do it?"

"Liz, you sure are the one who ought to know, if I could tell you, love."

And I sat up, too.

"Where's the vaunted conscience now?" Liz was saying, slowly and quietly.

"I'm no more of a soldier than I ever was, Liz, will never be a soldier. Hate strife and rifles and guns and how to handle them. They're quite against my nature still. At bayonet training, they try to brutalize you. They have to. No man in his ordinary day, or in any day that I can think of, wants to stick a bayonet into a pig, far less into a man."

Liz was determined to take this inert and unfeeling, but the effort was too much for her and at the last moment a shiver went through her and came out something like "Guu-urr!"

"It's not for the squeamish, and I'm squeamish, too. I don't — Liz, I don't ever mean to do it. I know myself that much, and myself says no to it. Plants a fixed foot. It would just have to be done on me, I suppose. But a man that doesn't like bullfighting never finds himself in the ring. So cheer up."

"You're still against it all, then?"

"I'm still against it all within myself, of course. But other chaps are, too. What I think of as conscience is that it's all no use to Australia. We're being killed for nothing. We've got to cross thousands of miles of sea to get to this war, and then there's so few of us that it's — that it doesn't affect their war very much at all. But it affects us. Why, nothing could persuade the bulk of Australians, as in 1914 or 1939, to turn aside from their peaceful lives — they're all living in peace, making no effort whatever — and wage war in Vietnam. So what others couldn't possibly be asked to do, why should we be asked to do? It's only because we're so expendably young. We don't need to be politically considered, and once we're in the army our mouths are shut, if only by ourselves. No politician has taken up our cause. You know why? Nobody thinks we have one or care about it ourselves. And he's frightened to press timid arguments and see all the other politicians laughing him bravely to scorn. But if the manhood of the nation feels no call to go, is it any wonder if we don't?"

Liz was listening to all this, and picking grass, and brushing it off her leg.

"I despise prime ministers that ask me to do this so that they can masquerade as a Great Power alongside the President of America. We're not a great power, and America won't make the mistake of thinking us so. She'll do what she wants in the end and won't consider us. Our country's just the same little pawn that the twenty-year-olds are. And what America's proving is that she maybe shouldn't show any power at all at any time in this part of the world. Once bitten, twice shy. And we're only doing this because we want her to be bitten, if necessary, for our sakes. And one thing more yet, pardon me, Liz?"

"Go on," she said. She didn't say, "I'll bear it," but she sounded like giving in. It was hard on Liz, all this, I know.

"We're not Asia and we're foolish to identify with it, or sort of seem to. Of course we're very involved with what happens there, but look at all the upset in Indonesia — far nearer, and we didn't meddle, and who now thinks, or ever thought, that we should have? Our influence isn't military presence, because we haven't the power and don't know ourselves yet."

"We've still got to make our own style," Liz said, bearing up. "But what about Limp?" she asked, stopping me from hectoring her. Very bad, very bad. Of me.

"Oh, Limp," I said, "Limp. He's managed better than he thought. It isn't as bad as he feared. He's soldiering at Wagga."

"But you got called up for him. Couldn't he — didn't he — why can't he go to Vietnam? If you're going?"

"Just that I'm going isn't reason enough." But I had to pluck my bit of grass there, for argument, too.

"You're mates, aren't you?"

"Oh, yes, we are, we were. But there's a difference. You see, Limp was being forced into the army. I didn't have to go on this trip. Well," I said, "I had to go, but that's no reason why he should have to."

"Very clear," said Liz.

"Well, Liz, he did come to me. Wretched, too. Said he didn't hold with volunteering. Never volunteer. Any old army hand will tell you that. And it's right enough. But I had to."

"Why?"

Liz was getting tired of this, but relentless, too: I

could hear. But I had to get out my cantankerous opinions, driven a bit, as I've been. I'm not at pains to be lily-white.

"Oh, then, let's not talk anymore, Liz, sweetheart. It's a thing that comes clear gradually. You've got to take up your own life by yourself more and more. I just know I've got to go through with this to the full. To the full," I said. "Pity, I know. But it's what they're making the fellahs do. Just some fellahs. God knows why. It's not thought out or thought about. But it goes on. And there are small paragraphs in the paper from time to time. And men are brought home when they're dead."

"Oh, don't," said Liz.

"I wouldn't want that," I said. "I'm against that, too. This enormous amends when you're nothing."

"What? Your folks. What about your dad?"

"Oh, let's not say. That's wretched. You see, though, Dad's in this peculiar position. He's taken himself out, which I don't agree with. So it gives him no right to speak and be considered when a serious matter crops up. You've always got to join in, be with everybody."

Well, it wasn't very pretty wooing that, but Liz had to hear about it. She was in it, she was involved, poor Liz, and I didn't want to involve her too much — if she could get by unscathed. But she didn't want to herself, I knew. Poor girl, she was helpless to alter the call-up thing. Maybe I did volunteer, but you're responsible, too. It's you that's separating young lovers up and down this country. It's in your name.

One day Liz said what was in her mind, as well as in mine.

"We might get married," Liz said.

"We might," I said, but instead I showed her a poem I'd been carrying in my pocket. "Liz," I said, "I'm going to leave you this."

She read it and was very upset, very. It was a love poem, but one to put an end to everything.

"Well, then," she said, after a long time, but impetuously, "if you won't marry me, you must love me true. I won't be balked of that for all my life. Be gentle with me."

And I was gentle with Liz, but she wept sore. I led her weeping off the beach and left her weeping on the shore of Sydney Harbour. Weeping anarchic Aphrodite? Love was no anarchy for us, but everything else was cruel and unkind. You needn't have pity for me, I've had my wish, but please look after Liz better. Don't send any more of the boys on such a squandering.

This writing that I've done in Vietnam is the best thing I could have done for Australia.

27

I'M NOT WRITING about the war. All I've done is to make a plea, and celebrate the life I should have been living, like you. If it all ends, as I end this section, with the love poem I gave to Liz, you can guess that I haven't got back, that's all. Don't let it trouble you. It's what your young folk are doing for you in Vietnam: you've sent them there for that. Only don't have me carted home to renew the grief of those that love me and shatter them over again. I'd sooner rest right here, and they'll acquiesce if they know it. You say we're a part of Asia, but I don't believe it — a part of the Earth, maybe.

I'm not fighting and dying for anything, you know — just doing what you say.

It's time you said better things, and deserved your young men.

Here's the poem that moved Liz and me a bit, gave us a kind of happiness.